T0146614

Second
CHANCE,
Again

NORMAN O'BANYON

SECOND CHANCE, AGAIN

This is a work of fiction. All of the characters, names, incidents,
organizations, and dialogue in this novel are either the products
of the author's imagination or are used fictitiously.

iUniverse books may be ordered through booksellers or by contacting:

iUniverse
1663 Liberty Drive
Bloomington, IN 47403
www.iuniverse.com
1-800-Authors (1-800-288-4677)

Because of the dynamic nature of the Internet, any web addresses or
links contained in this book may have changed since publication and
may no longer be valid. The views expressed in this work are solely those
of the author and do not necessarily reflect the views of the publisher,
and the publisher hereby disclaims any responsibility for them.

Any people depicted in stock imagery provided by Thinkstock are models,
and such images are being used for illustrative purposes only.
Certain stock imagery © Thinkstock.

ISBN: 978-1-5320-3805-1 (sc)
ISBN: 978-1-5320-3806-8 (e)

Library of Congress Control Number: 2017917892

Print information available on the last page.

iUniverse rev. date: 11/21/2017

Unless otherwise indicated, all scripture quotations are from The Holy Bible,
English Standard Version® (ESV®). Copyright ©2001 by Crossway Bibles, a
division of Good News Publishers. Used by permission. All rights reserved.

Everybody knows that the moon is white,
When we see it slide through the dark of night.
But what would you say if I said, "Hey,
I believe the side you can't see is pink?
It's not pale or dull, but happy I think.
Just like me there are two sides,
One that's plain and one that hides.
If you ask me which one I'd like to be,
I'd say the one that's pink and you can't see!"

I wrote that when I was in the third grade. Don't ask me what I was trying to hide from or express in a childish way. I think there was so much confusion around me I just wanted something to be understandable. Because I did know that my world was splitting into little pieces.

There had always been arguments; but when I was about three, they became shouting matches. Daddy's voice would get louder and mama's would get all screechy. I didn't know what was happening only that it was very bad. Then the seizures began.

"Daddy," Miky's little voice tried to break into their argument, "you'd better come look at Chrissy. She's acting weird."

When Jerry looked at his little daughter he immediately recognized a problem.

She was rolled in a tight ball with her little fists clenched on her chest and her face pulled back in a grimace. Her eyes

1

were open, but unfocused. She was rigid and unresponsive to his touch.

"She looks like she took some of mom's pills," Mike suggested, though he had no reason to think that.

Two or three minutes passed with no success in getting a response from the tiny girl. Finally Jerry scooped her up and headed for the General Hospital Emergency room.

A nurse carefully removed the shirt and shorts from the rigid body and she drew a small blood sample. At least a half a dozen different doctors examined Chrissy, looking everywhere for signs of abuse. Dr. Sherman finally said, "Jerry, this child is suffering a classic hysteria reaction. I have to ask you if you or anyone in the family have hit or harmed her in any way." His eyes were steady watching for any sign of avoidance.

"Nobody has hurt Chrissy in any way," the uncomfortable dad replied.

"I'm glad to hear that," the doctor said with a half smile. "But it does not explain why she is in the midst of such a severe reaction. Our natural instinct in times of challenge is either fight or flight. At twenty seven pounds she doesn't have a whole lot of fight in her, so she is trying to flee, to get away from some trauma. I'm guessing that you and your wife or girl friend have been in a noisy fight. Am I correct?" Again his eyes were piercing.

Softly Jerry replied, "Yeah, my wife and I have been ragging on one another because we can't seem to make our paychecks cover our debts and she's pregnant again."

"Well sir," the doctor sighed, "At the risk of adding to your problems, I must point out that by carelessly broadcasting your argument all over your family, you have added about twelve hundred dollars in emergency room expenses. I hope you have some insurance to cover that." There was no response from the dad.

"I put my earphones on your daughter about ten minutes

ago," the doctor reported. "Look what that simple thing has done." He pointed to a small body that was no longer contorted by anxiety, hands now comfortably relaxed and her eyes were closed. "She is hearing a disc called 'Celtic Twilight.' I play it when I need to stay calm in surgery. For a few dollars you could equip her to be less offended by your arguing. Better yet, how about getting some counseling with your wife so none of the others in your care have to put up with the bickering? I must tell you that we now have on file a record of abuse on Christina. If there is any more, the police will be notified."

Jerry thanked the doctor and assured him there would be no more emergency room trips. They shook hands and the dad carried a sleeping little daughter to the car.

While he could promise no more emergency room trips, he couldn't promise there would be no more fighting. I had two more hysteria reactions, one just before Ward was born and another when mom came home from work with a whisker burn. That's when daddy confessed he had had enough of this marriage.

He and Mike went to live somewhere else and Mommy and baby Ward and I lived with Nanny. There had been more and more screaming and crying and swearing and slamming doors and then they just went away. Nanny said they would probably be back. But that didn't happen. Mommy and I cried some, and then we just started to pretend that everything was all right, like the part of the moon you can't see is pink. She promised it would be all right. But it never was.

New men started to live with us as soon as mom found a new house for us to rent. Nanny was sick and I never saw her again. Ralph was the first. If I thought Daddy had been hard on us Ralph was lots worse. He liked to make me sit on his lap and he sort of wiggled around. He would put his wallet on the table and tell me, 'If you take a little I will give you a little.' Mommy called him sick and when he slapped Ward, she told him to get out and I had another reaction.

Then there was Tony who tried to be friendly with me. He rubbed my back, which was nice. He said he'd give me money if I was nice to him. Mommy told him to never come back.

The next loser was Gordy who smoked pot. He thought if we would breathe in the smoke too he could be more friendly with us. It was gross what he and Mommy would do, even when I was in the room with them. I had another reaction and the police arrested him. The judge put Mommy on probation.

Then there was Sean. Jeez was he mean. One day he tried to put his hand where it shouldn't be. He said if I could keep a secret he would show me something fun. Ward said he was creepy. Sean grabbed him and shook him like a toy. When he let go Ward fell on the coffee table and cut his chin and I had another reaction. The doctor reported that mean man to the police and Sean was history. Oh yeah, so was Ward. The judge put him in a foster home for his protection.

Rocco was the last of the men who came to live with us. He said that he was Mommy's manager. She worked nights for him. I'm pretty sure it was a bad job because she always took pills before she went to work. It was just after Christmas when the lady from Family Services came to our house. I guess Mommy was in jail for doing her job for Rocco. The judge told me I was going to be moved to an abused girl's shelter, so I ran away. When the police found me I was taken to Juvenile Detention. It helped me to think about the side of the moon that I can't see. You know, it is pink. Yes, it really is. At least it was something that I could believe.

After two weeks in detention I was taken to a big house in Shoreline where fifteen other girls lived with Cindy and Barb who were paid by the state. There were four rooms each with four bunk beds. Cindy cooked when Barb was the teacher and then they traded jobs. The one who cooked slept in her room in the back, the other got to go home to her own bed.

It didn't take me long to get used to the routine. We had time to do our school stuff, time to play in the yard on nice days, time to read and draw or anything else. The only trouble happened when I picked up stuff that didn't belong to me. If it was just lying around I thought it was finder's keepers. I was scolded and put in time-out a lot at first. One of the girls pointed out that I was an insult to the Lord because I was a thief but his name was inside Christina. I began to feel a reaction coming on so I went to my bed and tried to relax. I never thought that in all the profanity and cussing I had heard, my name was somehow mixed up with it. When I was feeling all clear, I asked Cindy if she would just call me Tina. Somehow it just seemed right not to be an insult to the Lord.

It's hard for a child to rebuild a family from the debris parents leave after a Demolition Derby marriage. Several of the girls left "the Home" to be in foster homes. I was hoping that someday I would too. After three years I asked Barb why I was not considered. "Is it because I steal stuff or lie?" I asked her.

"Oh no, Sweetie," she said to me. "Your case is different because of the abuse you suffered. The guidelines tell us that you can't be placed in a home with a younger boy. I know it's not fair, but it's for your protection."

Did you know that the part of the moon you can't see is pink? Her explanation didn't make sense either. It wasn't my protection they were worried about. They were afraid I might do something bad to the boy, like become a predator!

Homeschooling took me through the sixth grade and then the yellow bus stopped in front of our house for seven of us to go to Olympic Terrace Junior High School. It was extra nice to have some clothes that made us look normal and the opportunity to act normal. My grades were average or a little above, which was a good sign for home-schooling.

When I was in the ninth grade I overheard two guys at lunch talking about getting into the Smoke Shop after they closed. I didn't look at them or act strange, but when I got home I told Barb what I had overheard and she contacted the police. They caught those guys red-handed. We received a very nice letter from the Police Chief, who called us "Outstanding Citizens" and thanked us for the support we gave to the officers. He said we were helping to make our community one of honor and safety. I thought that was a little pink moon, but it felt very nice to do something truthful. It may have been the first time I received praise from someone with credibility. It wasn't a big deal. But on the other hand it was praise enough for me to stop stealing stuff because I wanted more of it. I wanted to be an honest helper of the community rather than an insult to the Lord.

I turned 14 the summer before I went to Fairwood High School. In most ways it would be the same old drag that I had been in. But this year I was given access to the computer so I could do classes on line too. The University of Nebraska offered an accredited home school for the high school level. Between the classes that I could attend at Fairwood and the computer course, I had hopes of better grades and maybe an early graduation so I could get a job. I signed up for an on-line Spanish introduction, U. S. History and English Literature.

That was also the summer that Trisha replaced Barb on the Home staff. Barb had accepted a nanny job for a UW graduate student. When I tearfully told her that I felt like some of my family was leaving me again, she told me that if I would like to come along with her some days during the summer break I could earn a little spending money as a baby sitter. It sounded a little pink moon to me, but at least it would keep her in my life, if for only a few hours each week.

As we drove up to the house she said, "Remember the mom's name is Lacey Tagawa. When I told her about my idea of having you as an assistant to help the children, she approved of it immediately. The boy's name is Mason, he's six and the girl's name is Madison, but they call her Maddy. She is four. The husband's name is Travis, but he is in Japan at the Nintendo offices right now. He's a computer whiz designing new games." It was my introduction to American family 21st century style. It would get even more strange.

As soon as Lacey greeted us she informed Barb that with this new summer schedule she had morning classes and a late afternoon class. "I'll try to be home by 7 o'clock, so you'll need to get the children up for breakfast as well as fix their supper too. Mason's Japanese is coming along well. His French is quite good, but I want you to answer only if he speaks to you in English. He's been getting rather lazy. Do you have any questions?" When Barb shook her head and assured the mom that we were in control, Lacey said, "There's cash on the counter for groceries and I'll transfer your pay into your accounts if you will provide me the numbers on Friday." Apparently she would see her children evenings and on the weekend. So began a summer of new responsibilities and understanding. It was also a time of discovery for me.

As the children finished their breakfast, Barb outlined a plan. "I think she will pay you as a babysitter, probably a dollar and a half an hour. She expects me to manage their entire day, so let's give you the task of being in charge of just one of them for a week at a time. If you begin with Maddy it will be easy for you to get to know them both, but I'll be responsible for Mason this week. Sometime we might all four play a game together. Mason is more advanced and might need more challenge than Maddy can follow. She has a big selection of books that she likes to hear over and over. I'll bet she has heard them enough to know them by heart."

Tina so hoped Barb was telling the truth. There was a hint of pink moon in the suggestion that she should not spend a week with Mason first

The children had bathed and put on fresh play clothes before breakfast. Now with the dishes cleared and their teeth brushed it was time to play. Maddy asked Tina if she would like to hear the story of the Magic Pony. Tina answered that she would like that very much. The happy four year old said, "Me too," as she handed the book to her new friend. "You can read this one and I'll read the next one." They read two more books from Maddy's shelf and she always agreed to read the next one. At ten o'clock Tina turned on the Nature channel and they watched a remarkable program about the Pacific Octopus.

When it was over, Tina had a quiz for Maddy: True or false: an octopus has a sharp beak like a parrot? (Correct answer is true.) How many legs does an octopus have, 4, 6, 8, 10? (Correct answer: 4 pair, 8.) How many eyes does an octopus have, 1, 2, 3, 4? (Correct answer: 2.) How many hearts does an octopus have, 1, 2, 3, 4? (Correct answer, 3.) How many bones does an octopus have, 10, 20, 30, none? (Correct answer: none) How does an octopus move from one place to another, crawl, swim, water-jet, all three? (Correct answer: all three.) How many spawning seasons does an octopus have, one, three, six, nine? (Correct answer: one.)

Maddy only missed one question and when it was explained that "spawning" means season to reproduce, she changed her answer to the correct one. "I felt sorry for the mama octopus who doesn't get to eat all the time her eggs are growing up. She dies of starvation to make sure they are safe and well." Tina was impressed with the comprehension of a four year old.

All through the lunch she wanted to retell the program to Mason, whether he was interested in an octopus or not. On their nice-day-walk around the block she was trying to tell Tina about her new pet octopus named Polly and the adventure she had when the ocean currents swept her away from the nice house she had lived in. It was quite an imaginary saga by the time they got back home. During drawing time she was supposed to draw her big idea for the day. Maddy created a giant octopus that could draw and color with all eight hands. With four she could start drawing in each corner and work toward the center. The other four added colors that started at the edges and got brighter toward the center. In her mind it was practically three dimensional.

On the way home, Tina was wondering if every day would be so filled with information. "I hardly caught a breath. That child seemed tireless."

Barb answered softly, "I've not seen that energy level from her. You must have caught her attention."

"The funny part is," Tina chuckled, "I probably learned more about octopuses than ever before. I'm still sort of revved up too."

"That is a super sign, Tina," Barb said with a wide smile. "If you were exhausted it would be difficult to get started in the morning. Do you have any notion what your subject will be?"

"I guess we'll see what's on the Nature channel." Tina laughed out loud, "As long as it's not about spiders we'll do just fine." But even as she said it she was convinced that darling little girl would be thrilled about it and they would have another fine day.

Later that evening Barb called to ask if Tina could be ready a bit earlier in the morning. Lacey had requested them to be there by 7:00 o'clock. She wanted to join a classmate for breakfast. "We can have granola with the kids," Barb assured her. "It will be a twelve hour day with a bonus."

Even though Tina thought it sounded like pink moon, she agreed to be ready.

When the dishes were cleared and teeth were brushed, Tina realized the bonus was going to be extra books for her to read for Maddy. "We've got lots of time to read the four new Berenstain Bear books that I haven't heard yet," the happy little girl declared. "Here's 'Mama's New Job.' That's a funny one about Mama Bear's quilt shop that takes all the time she used to have to help all her family. When she wasn't there, they learned that they could do the jobs themselves." Her happy innocent face convinced Tina that while the book was not unread, it was an anticipated pleasure.

A few minutes later, before they could finish talking about the beautiful patterns of the quilts, Maddy handed Tina another book saying, "'Go To the Doctor' is funny too because when Sister catches a cold and must go to bed, Papa Bear says that he never gets sick. Then Mama Bear gets a fever and must go to bed, Papa says that he never gets sick. When Brother gets a cough and sore throat, you just know what Papa is going to say." She chuckled in delightful anticipation. "Then the doctor has to come to their house because Papa is sick and in bed. He says, 'Well I almost never get sick.' Isn't that funny?" she asked as she fluffed her pillow preparing to hear Tina read the "new" book. Surprisingly Maddy's listening enthusiasm didn't fade, even when she produced yet another for Tina to read. It was titled "Trouble at School" and had the conclusion that it is never too late to correct a mistake.

"That reminds me of this last one you can read," Maddy said with a big smile. "It's called 'The Bears Get the 'Gimmies.' Daddy said it is about the bad choices some children make because they are greedy." Her voice became confidential as she said, "The last time mommy took us to the toy store, Mason had the Gimmies real bad. He wanted a construction set that had a battery powered lifter thing. His voice got all whiney and I thought he was crying. Mommy finally said he could have the set even though daddy said he was making a poor choice with such greedy behavior. I didn't think it was such a bad choice because as soon as I asked why he got two new things and I nearly cried, I got another one too. It seems like it was a good choice behavior."

Tina smiled as she answered, "Let's read it and see how the Bears act when they see other children act so childish." Several minutes later they were still talking about the story.

"Why do they call bad behavior 'childish'?" Maddy asked.

"I know that at times I misbehave, but so does daddy and for sure mommy does too. Are we all childish?"

"I suppose we are until we learn to make the best choices for the best reasons. It usually is clear to us when we see someone else do those embarrassing things. That's how we learn, just like the Berenstain Bears. I really like those books."

As Maddy was agreeing they heard Barb announce that the Nature channel program was about Brown Bats today. Mason had decided to join them and was already very interested.

When the captivating program was viewed, Barb asked, "What new thing did you just learn?"

Mason answered immediately, "Bats catch the bugs in the dark by 'echolocation.' That's cool. I never heard that word before. They make 20 calls a second until they find one. Then they make ten times that, 200 a second, as they close in and chomp on them." He seemed to find a ghoulish delight in describing the capture.

Maddy said thoughtfully, "They sleep almost all day and night, only awake for a few hours. What does 'hibunate' mean?"

Mason answered with a bit of attitude, "It's hibernate, silly. It means a longer deeper sleep like bears in the winter."

"Just think," Barb said, getting into the discussion, "they catch about four bugs every minute until their tummies are full."

Maddy had a sad face when she said, "They have a White Nose Sickness that is disappearing lots and lots of them. Maybe they are all going to the bridge in Texas. There must be a lot of bugs there 'cause there are lots of people watching them every night."

Tina said softly, "Here's a poem I wrote to help me remember how much I enjoyed that program:"

"Betty Bat sleeps all day and eats at twilight,
On bugs she catches while in flight.

She sings a little echo song for she can't see,
The tasty bugs that try to flee.
As many as 600 won't bite me, and can't get you.
She's happy when the hunting's through.
The work is over and she will rest with a nap or two."

Barb clapped her hands and complimented each observation. "This is so much fun," she said. "I'm already looking forward to tomorrow's. I wonder what it will be."

Mason quipped with a knowing smile, "Well you know these are all On Demand. We can watch them again or check on the ones we have missed."

Barb ruffled his short hair saying, "You wise guy. It's a gorgeous morning. Let's go for our walk and talk about this more. But first a bathroom stop." All four were smiling with such a happy morning.

At first Maddy wanted to talk about her pet bat that lived in her closet. She had to make sure that the window was left open every night so that she could go out and get back in when she was full. Her young imagination was at work when Mason explained all the hazards that were a danger to a night flyer. "There is a black and white cat, you know, that sits on the fence just waiting for Betty to fly by. That old cat would get her for sure," he said angrily, "if she wasn't so smart at flying."

Just before they completed their walk, Maddy asked for an explanation about poetry. "How do you make the words tell a story, but sound like a song without music?" she asked.

"It is very fun to choose words that sound alike, sort of like, 'glad' and 'had'" Tina explained, "Then use them in a story you want to tell." She thought for just a moment then said, "My bright pink balloon makes me glad. It's the biggest I've ever had. It's so big I need to stop, for one more puff will make it pop." She smiled at Maddy and asked, "Did you hear the story with rhyming words?"

The delighted child said, "Yes and I wish that story could come true. I'd love to have that big pink balloon."

All through lunch Maddy was coupling rhyming words: "bread, shed, head, bed; lake, bake, flake, shake; flower, hour, power, shower." It was entertaining and not quite irritating.

While they were still at the table, Barb introduced a new Chinese Checkers game. With minimal introductions and Tina and Maddy playing as a team, the first game was a learning experience. Mason was so hooked he insisted on a second, which Barb won again. The third game was really close. Mason contested that since Barb had begun the game she was a turn ahead of him. His argument was so convincing that he was given a final turn and also had all his players home. It was declared a tie and everyone was given an ice cream treat.

During her Drawing time Maddy's big idea picture was of a person sitting at a desk. She said it was her, writing poetry stories. Apparently her interest in bats was limited to their conservation. Perhaps her poetry might plead for their assistance.

Eight non-stop hours with the children is exhausting however the time is spent. Barb selected the video Fly Away Home for the children and Tina to watch as she prepared supper. A few minutes into the movie, Maddy was comfortably asleep against Tina's right side and Mason was gently leaning on her left side. They enjoyed the story of a young girl who rescues a flock of Canada geese. When it was over he said he liked tender movies that made happy tears.

After supper there were two more games of Chinese Checkers and they watched an old video of Lassie. It was finally time for the children to brush their teeth and get into pajamas. Tina read one more Berenstain Bear story before Lacey came home. The house was tidy and the children were happy to see her, but not as happy as Barb and Tina. It had been a very long day.

However, it set the pattern for the summer. It seemed that

Lacey frequently had breakfast appointments and was later than planned coming home in the evening. Tina had a nagging suspicion that there was some pink moon in Lacey's claim of school activities because Mr. Tagawa, Travis, came home for four summer weekends and Lacey didn't have any breakfast or evening obligations.

One afternoon Tina had an epiphany: Educated people often become wealthy; but wealthy people do not always act educated. Nonetheless, by Labor Day Tina had earned a bank account of over a thousand dollars and a wardrobe that allowed her to blend in with the other freshman girls. On those weeks when she had responsibility for Mason, she introduced him to backgammon and chess. She had learned the rules of both games just in time to teach them to her young student. At the same time she encouraged him to help her understand conversational French, which was on her autumn course list.

Barb had an idea that Tina gladly accepted if it could get approval from the Fairwood Guidance Counselor. If Tina could get a waiver to forego her gym class and study hall, her curriculum classes could be planned for mornings. She could be allowed to continue caring for the children from 12:30 until 7:30. After two meetings with Fairwood staff, the plan was approved. Lacey had made a standing appointment with a taxi to take Tina to the Tagawa Lake Forest Park home while her classmates went to lunch. If she had the endurance to work the plan, it would be colossal!

Through the autumn it was even better than that! Tina's grades were above average and Lacey had invited her to sort through a pile of her donation clothes since they were both a size 6. Tina had never imagined such abundance. Lovely slacks and sweaters, jeans and two sweatshirts, a warm coat and three party dresses filled a couple boxes. Lacey also announced that Travis would be home for two weeks in December. Barb and Tina were given vacation pay for that time and Tina was asked to sit with the kids on three occasions when the parents had evening plans. It was colossal indeed!

The final evening before Travis went back to Japan, he asked Tina, "Hey, tell me about this game you and Maddy made up. Is it as much fun as she said?"

Tina chuckled an answer, "Well it's not as much fun as Pac Man, but sort of on the same line and it is teaching Maddy to count." She thought for a moment. "We play on a checkerboard. Polly Octopus must stay away from the Nurse shark, a crab, and an eel. We roll one dice to see how many squares she gets to move. The first two rolls it's just Polly and the old crab. She starts from the middle and he comes after her from the edge. After two turns the shark comes in from another edge and he gets twice the roll of the dice. If she hasn't made it safely off the board, after two more rolls the eel comes from another edge. The game is over when she is either safely off the board, or captured for supper. The old crab can move diagonally, so it's not a very long game, but Maddy squeals a lots if she's Polly."

Travis was thinking how much fun it would be to create a larger computer field with more features. It would be fun to develop.

In retrospect, the four years of high school passed in a blur. Tina was either sleeping a few hours each night or studying, or caring for the children. Barb had a heart to heart talk with Lacey, stressing that her children needed more of a mother's attention. Maddy especially was suffering from those absent mornings and evenings. Lacey seemed surprised that her schedule might be challenged by one who provided childcare, but the extracurricular activity stopped and the effect on both children was obvious. She gave top priority to Maddy and Mason, which eased the schedule for Barb and Tina and proved that the part of the moon you can't see is pink.

Tina was flattered that Chip Stanley, a fellow student in her English Literature class, asked her out on two occasions. She explained in both cases that she had work obligations.

But it was delightful for her ego. There were a couple other phone conversations that were enticing for her, but always her priorities were very clear.

Finally, Lacey announced that she had passed her bar exam and was accepting a job in Japan. For Tina it was a bit like a death in the family. There could be no easing into the separation; they were moving by the end of the month. The prospect of a reunion was less than slim. As a farewell, eight year old Maddy presented Tina with a stack of Berenstain Bear books and ten year old Mason gave her his ivory chess set. She really didn't need anything to remind her of these precious children so she accepted them as one last act of affection.

Lacey presented her with a generous separation check and four boxes of donation clothes. Tina welcomed the check but was thrilled with the clothes. Wearing them caused her to look and feel like a new person. Lacey also gave Tina's name to a sorority sister living in central California. She told Tina, "Clara Meyers is a Biology professor at Cal State University, Chico, who is six months pregnant and in need of a live-in nanny housekeeper. Her husband is an ATF agent who is frequently gone on assignment. She is pretty vigorously looking for the right person. If you are accepted, you could attend some classes too and work on your degree."

Who could ever plan such a perfect scenario? By The time the Fairwood High School class of '93 graduated, Tina had flown to Chico for an interview weekend and with just three months left on her eligibility to stay in Miss Cindy's Shelter Home as a ward of the court she accepted a fresh chapter in her development. She liked the idea of living in sunny California.

When the green cab pulled up to the Ninth Avenue house, the kitchen door opened and a lady with an obvious tummy bulge hurried out. She wore a yellow cotton dress and had short hair. No, shorter than that! No, I'm talking buzz cut short! She had an enormous smile that accentuated her happy hazel eyes and as she approached the taxi she was saying, "You're here! You're finally here!"

As Tina stepped out of the cab, she started to say, "I'm Tin…

"Yes, I remember you. I know who you are," Clara said through laughter. "Lacey has told me over and over that you are going to be my little sister! I'm so glad to get to see you again." She embraced Tina warmly. "Come in! Your UPS stuff got here yesterday. That was so smart to send them rather than struggle with a bunch of boxes." Neither the smile nor warm greeting had lessened. "Your celebrity quarters are over the garage. May I get you a glass of juice or…" She was bursting with the hospitable greeting.

After a few minutes when that initial rush had settled down, Clara said, "Lacey told me repeatedly that you and Barb were the only reason she could finish her MBA and Law degree. You were life-savers for her." Clara's smile had turned serious, "With Bruce involved with 'copter training and mission assignments, I didn't know how I'd get through the next few months without you." A tiny tear slid down her cheek emphasizing the truth of her words. "Until now I was afraid I would have to do it alone. This big old house had a makeover before we bought it. Even with all the modern bells and whistles, I felt pretty overwhelmed."

Tina realized how lonely this pregnant lady seemed in her husband's absence.

"Then you understand my situation," she said softly. "You understand that this is like a second chance for me. I am really glad for this job and the help I can be to you. I'm grateful for a stable righteous home so I can be of assistance." She was still for a moment then added, "and the possibility of doing some undergraduate classes at the same time is just cream on the top."

Clara asked, "Do you think you can finish your degree in four or five years?" She was unwilling to think about a limited experience with Tina right now.

With a snort, Tina chuckled, "Maybe it will take six or seven years. I just hope I can work at it in our spare time."

"I love the idea of our time," Clara said warmly as she embraced Tina again. "I believe we have plenty of that to achieve your goals. Monday I will introduce you to our registrar. We still have a week to sign up for the summer session. I believe she will allow you to enroll as a family dependant because you are living with me." Both women embraced the other again not knowing the wishful thinking of their words. She offered Tina a sheet of paper with a list of daily expectations and chores. It was going to be so workable!

A bit later, as Tina was unpacking her things, she understood why Clara had called it "celebrity quarters". Over the garage, it was a huge apartment with a full bathroom, a queen sized bed in a cozy room. There was a sink and a microwave, a study desk and a small table. She even had a sofa and her own TV. It was wonderful! Her anxious thoughts about the future were evaporating. In fact her future had more opportunity than she had dreamed; gone were the ghosts of a broken home, the shelter home and dependence on others who she had not chosen. This was the first time in her life that Tina felt truly in control of her destiny. She whispered a prayer of gratitude.

Nine learning, adjusting, happy days later, Bruce returned from his training session. Tina was impressed with the tall (he was 6'3") tanned athletic man. His laughter was contagious and his smile captivating. Tina knew she was going to love this family. After a cheery reunion and introduction, he began to relax and unload the tensions he had been carrying. The new helicopter was state of the art technology, which allowed him to speak in terms they scarcely understood. But it was clear that he felt fortunate to be assigned as its pilot.

After a pleasant supper and chilled beer, he became even more talkative. "We don't worry as much about the people sneaking into the U.S.," Bruce said casually. "If we can turn them around we do, but they are no immediate threat. But we struggle trying to keep out the drugs. That is a threat and there seems to be no end to the ingenious ways they bring it in." Even though it was an unfinished mission, he began to tell Clara what he had been doing. "That Bell Super Cobra is a dream to drive," he said after drinking another Shasta Amber. "It is so much more efficient than the old birds we flew in the desert. The squad hit a Mexicali drug strong house. They were caught by complete surprise. We had no casualties and after the explosion and fire there was no way to count their losses. It was amazing. We were told that a ranking splinter group of the Guerra's had just left and was hiding up in Wasco, but by the time we got there they were gone. That Cobra is an amazing aircraft. We'll catch up with them next time."

Tina wasn't sure how much of his casual report was appropriate for her ears. But his buoyant lack of secrecy helped her feel like a member of the family. She sipped her diet coke wondering how much trouble he would be in if his superiors knew that he was sharing this information.

Bruce may have realized he was being overly talkative, or he may have just run out of news to tell. In either case he changed the subject abruptly, asking Tina if she had a driver's license. When she shook her head, he told her it would be his privilege to teach her the fundamentals and get her the manual so she could take the test. "In Clara's third trimester, it will be important to have a duty driver on hand when I'm not here."

Then sounding like a teacher he began to help her understand her new city. "Big Chico Creek sets the northwest southeast layout of our streets. That small stream is from the convergence of the Cascade and Sierra Mountains. We are on the north side of it called the Avenue district. The five main avenues are named after trees: Chestnut, Hazel, Ivy, Cherry and Orange. You probably noticed that the first letters of those spell Chico. Cool, huh?" His smile expressed a relaxed satisfaction. "We are at 9I, or ninth and Ivy. A couple trips through it and you'll understand how easy it is to get around. We are only two blocks north of the campus."

On one hand it was a busy summer. Tina was up each day early enough to scramble Bruce some eggs for breakfast, or fix his favorite, Poached eggs on corned beef hash. She had a summer session Spanish class that was from 9 a.m.to 4 p.m. but earned a full year's credit. In warm June she passed her driver's test on the first try. July was pretty hot and she developed a nice assortment of entree salads that were both delicious and cooling. Clara especially liked the Taco salads. In smokin' hot August Tina barbequed outside. To Bruce and Clara's delight she presented smoked lemon salmon as well as her own original bacon soy sauce steak. She also tried to copy the menu of the Red Robins exotic burgers.

Bruce was on overnight assignments twice in June, twice in July with an additional three nighter. He was only gone for one August overnighter, but there was a quad night that worried Clara, because she had some contractions. Fortunately it was a false alarm. But one that demonstrated Tina's proficiency in dealing with an emergency and her ability to navigate directly to Memorial Hospital. The trio was relieved that it had been a drill and grateful for Tina's assistance.

Labor Day was appropriately named. Just before 4 a.m. Clara woke Bruce saying, "Honey, I'm pretty sure it's time to go." A little after 2 p.m. Jewel Maria was born.

Tina understood without being told that her job description had just changed. Now, instead of caring mainly for Bruce, she had to care for Clara's needs and Jewel's too. She would try to maintain the household as well as shopping and preparing the meals, so it would be seamless. She knew that she could make this house a gentle place of joy.

The fall quarter began a week later. Her conference with Mrs. Russell the registrar, requested afternoon classes so Tina could care for Clara and the baby in the mornings. The plan was still going to work; it was just going to take a little more effort. Her class schedule was, first year French where she would learn how much she had acquired from Mason; Political Science 101; Business Principles; and English Literature, which would require a ton of reading. She smiled secretly because she had most of every morning for reading.

"Hi, is this seat taken?" He was pleasantly courteous and friendly at the same time. Tina thought she remembered him from the French class.

"Help yourself," she smiled. "It pays to be prompt at lunch, before it gets crowded." She continued to read the chapter on Office Management.

"Hi,' he repeated. "I'm Nick from your French class. Are you new to Cal State?" His light blue eyes were steady on hers and for a moment it felt like they were friends.

"I am." She took another bite of tuna sandwich and said after a couple chews, "There is a ton of reading to keep up with the assignments."

"Forgive me for interrupting you. It's just that you are the most lovely girl in this cafeteria that will speak to me." He took a large bite of his sandwich as Tina glanced at him.

Several bites later she said, "I'm Tina. I'm nanny for Mrs. Meyers since she just had her baby. Trying to work and study at the same time is a challenge."

"You see what a nice person you are?" the young man asked happily. "Most girls would be rude and tell me to take it to a different table, but you explained why you don't have time to return my compliments. I'll be quiet now, but will you be here tomorrow? Perhaps we could have another lunch together while you read more." His smile was genuine as he took a final bite.

She tried hard for the remainder of the afternoon to ignore that brief conversation. Try as she might, his happy face and clever conversation sneaked into her awareness again and again. She would deny it, but down deep she was happy for Nick's jovial wit and words.

At dinner Bruce explained that reliable eyewitnesses had spotted the Guerra's up by Butte Meadows. Tina asked if "Guerra" was Spanish for "warrior." Bruce confirmed that it was, then added, "There is an anti-government group of young radical survivalists that call themselves by that name. The list of crimes and complaints committed by them is embarrassing. We've chased them from Tijuana to Redding. This tip is from near Plumas Nation Forest and the terrain up there is too broken to depend on the chopper moving us so we're taking a caravan with the squad from Fairfield joining us. Depending on what we run into, I should be home by supper."

That was so optimistic. The five car column had no trouble the first part of their journey. The four lanes were wide open. But when they got to the narrow winding hill country their pace was complicated. First a 40's Ford pickup slowed them by driving 35 mph in a 55 zone. It was impossible to pass in the curvy blind areas. After he turned off, it was a flat bed loaded with hay moving ponderously. It took them almost two hours to get to the junction. The slow pace prevented any sort of surprise and gave the Guerra's plenty of time to either escape or plan an ambush.

Just before Meadows, the convoy turned onto a dusty fire service road, which soon had them travelling even more slowly through a cloud of dust. The front car suddenly drove over a spike strip hidden in the dirt. Tires were destroyed! At the same time, men hidden by brush beside the road and the blinding dust pulled a spike strip behind the tires of the end car that would try to back out of the ambush. More tires were destroyed and effectively the progress of the column was stymied. The team was trapped so Major Marsh ordered the agents out of the transports and begin a systematic advance on foot in the protection of trees and brush.

It was well after noon when the first shot rang out from the hillside. The agents found cover but they could see no target to return fire. After a few minutes Major Marsh ordered them to move out carefully. Fifteen minutes later another report sounded from a grove of trees on the opposite side of the road and once again the agents sought cover but had no visible enemy. Stop, go, take cover, wait; it was ridiculous.

The road twisted around a curve and came to a field of rock rubble on both sides, where visibility was improved. Major Marsh ordered double time with weapons drawn. When they topped the next ridge they could finally see their objective about a half mile further. There was open terrain all the way. At a gate, the lead agent was about to open the metal hasp when a bullet hit his Mylar vest and knocked him down. A barrage of fire came from the two story building, bullets striking all around them. There were four minor wounds.

"Screw this!" the Major growled. He radioed the base for some air power, giving coordinates. Twelve minutes later an F-18 flew overhead dropping a small smart bomb that targeted the laser-painted building. Instantly it was turned into a smoking heap of splinters and debris. There was, of course, no more defensive fire; the summer meadow was once again still. With nearly a dozen agents examining the rubble they found sparse evidence. They uncovered six bodies that would be taken to Sacramento for identification, but the one known as "Sak" was not one of them. Regrettably there were no documents or information useful in the hunt for the rest of the Guerra's. With all this day's engagement, there were only a few small caliber weapons to show for their efforts. But it would be considered a victory in defense of our government even though there would be no mention of it in the newspaper other than the report of a natural gas incident in an abandoned building. It took four hours for the team from maintenance to replace all the destroyed tires so it was after 1 a.m. before Bruce could quietly return to his cozy home.

"May I fix you a couple bacon and egg burritos?" Tina asked the sleepy man. "I heard you come in late last night. I'll bet you had a rough day." She wouldn't ask about it but was determined to help make this a more pleasant morning.

"What I need most," Bruce said with a husky voice, "is a stout cup..." She slid a mug of coffee in front of him and a creamer to fix it just the way he liked it. After a couple strong hits, he added, "Tina, I agree with Clara. You have been a blessing to us. We thought the baby would be a complication. While it has changed her teaching schedule for a couple months, this house is a model of efficiency thanks to you." She served him a plate with some morning nourishment and a smiling curtsy in response.

Clara joined them, her short hair growing out to a jumble of new curls and her sleepy eyes on the coffee pot. As Tina poured her a cup and offered the creamer, Clara asked, "Was it worse than you planned? You got home pretty late."

"Yeah it was real messy. Those sorts of days remind me why we call it a 'war on drugs.'"

She leaned over placing her cheek on his shoulder. "Were there casualties?" she asked softly.

"None of our team was injured seriously; but we blew an old farmhouse and half dozen angry young men into smithereens." His voice sounded weary.

She kissed his cheek and whispered, "I'm sorry you must do that. I know it is not in your nature."

He turned so he could return the kiss gently on her lips. "Yeah, but you know what they say: It's like changing diapers. Somebody has got to do it." Then a bit brighter he said, "I just received a call from a couple fellows who have a gangbuster idea that would get me out of the war business." They both enjoyed their morning coffee.

"Hi Tina," Nick's soft voice made her flinch with surprise. "I hope I can join you for lunch. I brought a psych book so at least our brains may be joined." His smile was familiar but his boldness, in this case, reminded her of some of those nasty men her mom had brought home.

She folded her book, dropping it into her carrying bag and placing her sandwich in it too. Smiling only a little she said softly, "Maybe your brain can do it alone." She turned away from a surprised young man who had thought he had made a better connection than this rejection. The worst part was it had been witnessed by several women sitting nearby. He sat and ate in silence.

A few minutes later he apologized before their French class began. "I'm sorry if I offended you. I was trying to be charming," he said with his boyish smile. "It seems I need to work on that."

Tina looked at him directly and said softly, "Nick I am not interested in being worked on or joined with you. I am here to work and get an education. Anything else is a distraction." She sat down at her desk. "Perhaps you should try some of the sorority girls; oh wait, they don't eat in the cafeteria."

October ushered in little Jewel's first month day, celebrated by a tender baptism service at the Foursquare Church. There was a full array of new subjects for Tina to learn and Bruce's folks came to visit for Thanksgiving week. Before Tina knew it the first quarter was over and she had earned a 4 point in all her classes. Clara's folks helped bring in a happy 1994 new year.

Mrs. Russell requested a meeting with Tina. Apparently the administration was aware of her excellent first quarter and wanted to help her while assisting Mrs. Meyers back to full time. "Come in Tina. Have a seat. We are so proud of your remarkable accomplishment so far this school year." When she was seated, the registrar continued. "Tell me if you have any class request for the spring."

Tina shrugged and said, "Your suggestion for a translator career sounded interesting. I am now competent in both Spanish and French. I've given some thought to adding Arabic or Russian, but I think getting the required subjects out of the way might be a wiser tactic." Her relaxed smile showed Mrs. Russell that she would welcome any suggestion.

"Well, to graduate you will need at least one year of a science. Biology, geology or zoology can satisfy that. They each have interesting first years, and evening laboratories. Zoology is the only afternoon science class and there are three of those. Also, if you are interested, a Russian 101 intensive is going to be offered in the evenings. In four months you could earn a whole year's credit." In a very short time a plan was formed that would take her through her sophomore year. She loved her home, had a growing bank account and was well on her way into a college education. What was not to like with that picture?

"Hi. My name is Nick. Is this seat taken?" His shy smile only amplified his polite manner.

"You are welcome to sit here but I will warn you that I need all the study time I can use. Sometimes I get grouchy if others pester me." The words were not spoken harshly, but Nick was warned and he knew she meant it. He twisted so he could read the book she was reading. "Ooooh, you are in Russian 101."

"You are familiar with the book. Did you take the class?" Suddenly the interruption took a less irritating tone.

"Yes I did, but not by choice. My father teaches the course."

"Really," she replied. Dr. Akimov is your father?" When the young man nodded, she continued, "French and Spanish were alike in so many places I had less challenge with them. But Russian is completely different. I'm beginning to question the wisdom of signing up for the intensive."

"My dad's old computer has a vocabulary program that translates English into Russian. If you provide me with a thumb drive, I'll be happy to share a copy with you. Maybe that would earn me a smile of appreciation." His smile was a bit too victorious for Tina's comfort so she said, "I'll pick one up at the bookstore one of these days." She closed her book and was about to stand.

Nick said quietly, "Please don't go. I won't say another word. I don't want to offend you. Just the opposite; I want to be your friend." His eyes searched hers.

Tina relaxed and said, "How is that not saying another word? Stop trying to be such a sleazy hustler all the time. It does not honor you. My appreciation is not up for trade, I don't care what you are offering. I'm giving you this second chance because I would like to be your friend." Her smile didn't warn him that her sentence wasn't quite ended. "But not your conquest."

He gulped, blinked and shook his head. Several women nearby had overheard a loaded word. "That I clearly understand," he said quietly as he began eating his sandwich and she walked away.

Wednesday evening he was waiting outside the classroom. Nick offered her the thumb-drive saying, "I hope this helps you as much as it did me." She didn't walk passed him, so he asked, "It's getting pretty dark. Would you mind if I walk you home? We live at O13 so it is on my way." His warm smile was welcome and the prospects of having someone with her was even more so.

As they walked across the campus, Tina asked, "How did you come to live here? Your folks have a heavy accent but you sound like a native." She thought talking about his family might be a little less personal for her.

Her walking companion was delighted in her interest. "My Grandfather, Nicolai, was instrumental in designing the first wave of Khrushchev's 1953 Thaw, as it is commonly called. It was an effort to learn about American culture and economics.

My father, Grigori, was 24 when he came to the U.S. He wasn't a spy exactly, but his purpose was information gathering while he was a guest professor at Cal State Fullerton. My mother, Dorset, joined him two years later and they were married almost immediately. It may have been an arrangement; I was never told about that.

"In '59 following the Cuban missile crisis, Gorbachev's glasnost policies left many teachers stranded here so eventually my folks were granted citizenship. My brother, Soren, was born in '66, and I came along in '72. They thought it was clever to name me Nicholas in honor of the Christmas saint. I think it was in '75 that they came here. Chico needed a coach for the women's gymnastics. Since my mother competed in the '56 Olympics she was a top choice."

Tina could see her house across the street. With one more question she would be home safe and sound. "Does your brother live here with you?"

If Nick was aware of her filibuster he gave no sign of it. "No. Soren was part of a student protest in his freshman year. His name means 'god of war,' appropriately because he destroyed some property and was arrested. Now he works for a Bay area construction company. I haven't seen him for a couple years." He shrugged as she pointed to her house. "Or more," he finished the sentence. "May I walk you home after class tomorrow?"

Tina patted him on the shoulder saying, "We'll see. Thanks for the escort." She walked up the driveway before he could answer her.

When Tina plugged the thumb drive into the computer's USB port she expected a dictionary file. What she found were 28 files! That airhead Nick had copied his father's entire hard drive. There were even papers that Soren had written for his classes twelve years ago. What a waste. She copied the dictionary to her own hard drive and tossed the thumb drive into her desk drawer.

Just after Easter a large gold letter "G" graffiti tag was sprayed on the side of the Red Bluff National Bank. It was quickly removed, but three days later that bank was robbed by three men wearing hoods. They warned that if a dye pack was used there would be severe retaliation. The Guerra were declaring war on the establishment. That same thing happened at the Yuba City bank in July and the Woodland bank in September. Local and state police as well as FBI teams were fielding and following information on the crimes. Finally, on October 12th the Sacramento team had solid information that the group called "G" was using a house on the outskirts of Marysville. A combined strike force, including the Chico ATF, would investigate.

Major Marsh shared the part of the battle plan that was Chico's responsibility. "We have the right flank. We're going to stand off at least a hundred yards because the FBI brought their Remington M2 50 caliber attack rifles. Those can shoot clear through the house unless they hit a fireplace," he reminded them. "You don't want any friendly fire. Brooks, take the back corner. Meyers the side and Walsh, the front corner. Remember you have friendly's on your twelve. Let's be extra careful with this one." They took their positions and waited.

A loud speaker announced, "This is the FBI. We have a warrant to search the house. Come out peacefully." Before the words were finished, an upstairs window was broken and a rifle shot hit the side window of one of the shielding cars. A downstairs window also burst out so a rifle could shoot at another.

The heavy growl of the Remington's drowned out the other reports, if there were any. In thirty seconds there were nearly four hundred rounds slammed into the old farm house. There was a belch of smoke from the back of the house and an explosion that marked the end of the effort. Either a small bomb, a propane tank or a stash of ammunition had been hit by a 50. Caliber round. No further sounds came from the house so after a couple minutes an officer wearing heavy protection went to the door and pushed it open. There was no other resistance.

A quick scan by the FBI forensic team counted seven bodies; five adult males, an adult female and a juvenile male. Because a small fire in the kitchen was growing with no attempts to control it, the bodies were quickly removed for identification in Sacramento. A few weapons were confiscated, and a desk drawer-full of papers would be examined later. Once again the news would report the burning of an abandoned farmhouse. This one, however, would generate retaliation.

Once again Bruce was relaxing at the table following a delightful supper. "I don't know how you do it," he chuckled. "Every day you come up with great meals and you make it look easy." Clara smiled a warm agreement.

Major Marsh's debriefing had tried to put a positive spin on the events of the day. Finally here, with his family, Bruce was able to say, "It was like a horror movie, even though we were just by-standers. They may have fired a couple rounds at us, but once again our fire-power was brutal. That old farmhouse was turned into splinters in less than a minute." Tina thought he was about to cry. "But when they found the bodies of a woman and a nine or ten year old boy, I knew it was just wrong." The room was suddenly still and chilled. Tina thought of the only ten year old boy she knew, Mason.

Finally Bruce managed a half smile. He said, "This afternoon made me think how nice it would be to become a flight instructor." He squared his shoulders and said much more brightly, "Tina, how do you come up with these interesting meals. I don't know anyone who eats as well as we do every darned day." His appreciative smile suggested an answer would be welcomed.

"Well, I like to watch the Food Channel," her soft voice replied, "when I am doing the laundry. There's a show called 'Semi-homemade.' The lady uses canned or prepared food off the shelf. She has a way of combining those with fresh vegetables, rice or noodles. Then she comes up with dishes that seem very complicated but are done in just minutes. So she gets the credit for being the good cook."

Now letting that smile grow again, Bruce said, "Well, I'm all for passing the credit around as long as these menus continue. You're doing a marvelous job and Clara says you're bagging some great grades at the same time. Super!" He was indeed passing the credit around.

Before they left the table, Clara asked, "Have you heard any more from the fellows who were talking about a different career path? It feels to me that doing war against civilians doesn't go down very well. Have you given any more thought to something else?"

"As a matter of fact they have called me twice this winter. They have a concept of bringing Japanese golfers here for vacations. It is still vague, more like a pipe dream. He thinks there are hundreds of them who would gladly pay big bucks. It just needs someone who can organize it."

May brought finals and once again Tina was pleased with her accomplishments. She signed up for a summer intensive, second year Russian, taught by Mrs. Akimov. But the achievement most pleasing to Tina was Jewel's. She had learned to pull herself up and stand beside the sofa. Now all the stairs had safety baby gates.

"Tina, with school out for the summer. Bruce and I are going to take a vacation for three glorious weeks. We want to see his folks in Virginia City and mine in Seattle." Her face beamed as she said, "A coast to coast excursion with Jewel. We've been getting pressure from the grandparents, even though I pointed out that it would be easier for them to come here. If you have family in Washington that you would like to visit, we would be happy to help with travel expenses."

Tina smiled shyly and answered, "Thank you. That is

super generous of you. I think I told you that our family disintegrated when I was real little. I have no one to visit, but Mrs. Russell has already talked with me. She suspected that I would be available for a Political Science session and a Human Resources afternoon class, which will keep me busy. If you trust me, I'll hold down the fort here." Her smile bloomed into a grin.

"Of course we trust you," Clara said as she gave Tina a happy hug. "We just don't want you to burn out, so by all means, do what is best for you."

It was a sound plan and the one who enjoyed it the most was Nick. He could work his job with the Highway Department, take a shower and change clothes, grab a bite to eat, drive to the Meyers home and walk across the campus and be outside the Russian classroom in time to walk Tina home. He was thoughtful and courteous, although the two times he tried to hold her hand she informed him that she needed no assistance. When he suggested that with such a big empty house he could come in for a while just to keep her company, she told him that was a ridiculous idea and he could discontinue the evening escorts. He understood her boundaries and respected them, grudgingly. He finally had to accept the fact that romance was not in Tina's agenda.

The travelers returned, saying again and again how good it was to be home. Tina was in total agreement. She had been surprised how much she missed that toddler. Clara said several times that she was taking more attentive care than Jewel's mom. Yes, it was good to be home.

Warm September ushered in another football season and a fresh round of subjects for Tina. Without a language intensive, she signed up for two evening classes and three easy afternoon classes, one of which was second year French. Now she would know how much assistance Mason had been. It also ushered in the ominous season of retaliation.

The evening news carried the story of an assault in the State

House parking garage. "Early reports tell us of the ambush of the Associate Director of the FBI by two men with handguns. Several shots were fired and Mr. Franklin was taken to the trauma center with serious but non-life threatening wounds. He is expected to recover. There is a possibility that this assault may be connected to an ongoing case. A paper was dropped on his bleeding body. It stated, 'Remember Marysville,' and bore a large orange letter G."

All law enforcement agencies in California were on high alert even though it seemed they were looking for a ghost. No new information came for two months. At supper Bruce was growling about the puzzle. "We've believed that the Guerra's were from Latin America. Of the thirteen recent Guerra casualties we've identified seven with Russian connections. We've been looking in the wrong direction. We need to revisit our overlooked Russian leads, maybe some old documents we've discarded or neglected." Perhaps that remark caused Tina to recall the thumb drive. She had pondered if there was anything more she could do beside making sure Bruce had a good breakfast and a quiet evening. She asked him, "Would you think a copy of Professor Akimov's computer would help? That might have some interesting files?"

Bruce shook his head and replied, "Probably not because it is so dated. But I would rather scan for some new leads than lose another cribbage game." He chuckled as she hurried out to her room to see if it was still in the drawer.

When the thumb drive was finally booted up, it was clear that these were very dated and of little interest. They had been sorted alphabetically. Twenty seven seemed of no importance. But when he saw the title of the last one a shiver ran down his back. It was subject titled, "Warriors"!

"Oh Tina," he whispered as he opened the file, "this is hot. This has some names and phone numbers. May I take this in to the office in the morning? I'll bet there will be a lot of folks who want to see what this might tell us. Good job! Wouldn't it be amazing if the one who is the best cook among us is also the key to cracking this thing wide open?" He gave her shoulder a pat and a friendly squeeze.

Tina remembered so long ago when the chief of police's letter had made her beam with happy pride. This was so much better!

For days all Bruce could talk about was the growing list of suspects. Already five of the names had matched men who had been killed either at Butte Meadows or Marysville. It was obvious the list was very important to find the leader of the Guerra's.

The day after Christmas Major Winslow Carre, commander of the Fairfield AFT squad, was enjoying a holiday break with his family at their lakeside cabin. Just six miles north of Vacaville, it was such a peaceful retreat that even his teenage daughter had few complaints. But just about midnight that serenity was shattered as two flaming Molotov cocktails were thrown through the front windows. The blaze would have been fatal for them if the third one thrown through the back door would have ignited. Because it didn't, the family was able to exit safely, even the family dog. They did hear a voice shout, "Remember Marysville!" so there was little doubt who created the inferno. The spreading fire that threatened several nearby homes, took the rest of the night and all the next day for the volunteer fire department to extinguish.

Information from the thumb drive was not only helpful in identifications; two of the files were instructions for making and placing a poison gas bomb. The ingredients were antiquated but alarming. This was far more than political unrest. This was out and out terrorism!

An analyst pouring over the files discovered that Soren Akimov often just used his first initial. Sak! He had been implicated in two of the house raids and a bank robbery. It was another significant piece of the puzzle because now they had a specific target to find.

Lecture by lecture, book by book, test by test the winter passed and once again Tina was satisfied with her effort. A couple easy summer sessions would complete her sophomore year. Half done!

"Tina Sweetie, may I ask a favor from you?" Clara's voice was so dear to her and the possibility of doing anything that was needed was welcome.

"Of course," she cheerily answered. "What may I do to help you?"

"I have an early morning doctor's appointment. It's nothing serious but I'll need a bit of anesthesia. Could I ask you to go along with me and watch Jewels for a bit, then drive us home?"

"Yes, of course I'm happy to help. Are you having some surgery?" It was the first Tina had heard about a problem.

"Not surgery, exactly," Clara really was comfortable talking about it. "It's more like repair. We've been talking about another child and this little tuck might make that possible." There was a bit of a flush on her cheeks and Tina had no way of knowing whether that was a shy blush or a happy rush. In either case it was sweet. "We'll need to get an early start. Brucey has said we should take his car, the Crown Victoria; there is more car seat room in it than my Fiesta."

There were so many factors that contributed to the following minutes:

They went out the kitchen door into the garage so they missed seeing the gold colored "G" sprayed on their front door;

The dark privacy covering on the Ford's windows concealed who or how many were in the car:

They were focused on a sleepy little girl as they turned onto Ninth so they missed the car that pulled out from the curb and followed them;

They turned onto one way Oroville Avenue and the following car pulled up beside them and neither noticed the window roll down. There were so many danger signs they didn't see because of the happy morning.

The loud gunshot made Tina scream and Clara grab her neck as a fountain of blood splashed on the dash and windshield which had a hole where the bullet had exited. The shooter was firing blind through the privacy glass. A second spurt of blood told them that arterial bleeding was an urgent crisis. Clara bent forward to take the car out of gear and stepped on the emergency brake. As Tina bent over to draw a diaper out of Jewel's bag, a second gunshot shattered the side window and struck Clara behind her arm into her chest. A third shot was fired straight toward Tina. It hit the door frame instead and the entire driver's side window collapsed.

Tina was reaching to place the diaper as some sort of containment against the steady tide of bleeding when her eyes met those of the driver beside them. Recognition was immediate for both. Nick Akimov jerked the wheel away in a moment of understanding that these were not their intended target, or perhaps it was fear of identification. They were after the ATF officer Meyers. Or possibly it was his affection for the lady who had allowed him to walk with her all year through. The maroon Honda disappeared down a side street as the Ford came to a stop and Clara murmured, "Take care of th…." She slumped onto Tina's lap as the terrified woman called 911 for assistance. She had a momentary sensation of a reaction coming on, but by sheer will power refused to allow it. Then she called Bruce, sharing the terrible news through her sobs. He assured her was on his way; he would be there as quickly as possible

It only took the ambulance three minutes to get to them, but that was three minutes longer than Clara lived. Both Tina and Jewel were hysterically crying when the emergency vehicle arrived. A Chico police cruiser was only a minute later and a crowd of curious people gathered on the sidewalk. Tina was trying to pull herself together enough to give an accurate statement to the patrol officer when Bruce arrived. He first ran to the covered body on the gurney. It was true! His delightful, gentle, intelligent loving partner was gone. As tears flowed down his cheeks he turned to Tina and Jewel. First he examined the child to assure himself that she wasn't injured; then he noted the dozen or so small bleeding punctures on Tina's face from the glass shards. He embraced and thanked her for trying to help Clara. Their sobs joined uncontrollably.

Time seemed irrelevant in light of their loss. Minutes seemed like hours. Finally Major Marsh arrived with Chaplain White. They had to hear the gruesome account now from the standpoint of the larger issue of the Guerra's. The rest of the flight crew arrived and the Chaplain said quietly, "Now is the time for grief, not thoughts of vengeance. We can find stability by claiming memories of Clara's wondrous vitality, her laughter, joy and affection, the way she loved to dance barefooted on the carpet. Now is a time to remember that you are not alone in this unthinkable loss." He was trying to shift their focus from the grizzly scene to one of treasured reflections. "Hear this prayer; "God of Mystery and Mercy, we open our hearts to you because we feel so empty in this tragic moment. You promised to never leave us desolate, so we lift our emptiness to your fullness, our pain to your peace. Lord, comfort us in this hour that we may accept the fact that we can never change what has happened here this morning, but we can control how this affects us. With your strength growing within us, we shall choose this moment of grief to temper our resolve to honor Clara's memory and bring justice to those who have committed this terrible crime; strengthen us to be your swift sword of righteousness.

"We are mindful of the immediate family of Clara's who especially need your Heavenly Comfort today and the days to come. Remind them that she is not lost. She rests gently in your hand. Even as you restore peace after a storm, so will you bestow a renewed quietness through your peace-instilling presence that is surrounding us even now. We ask this in the name of him who gave his very life for us, Jesus, our Lord. Amen."

Major Marsh gave a workable plan for the next few hours. "Mr. Meyers you will follow the ambulance to Memorial. The first difficult task will be the permission for organ donation. Later in the day you can talk with Chaplain White about a funeral home and the sort of service Clara wanted. You will take the week off to make those arrangements and talk with family folks who will be heart-broken too. We will have the Ford towed to the base where the police can examine it if they need to, and we can have the glass replaced.

"Miss Winter, the Chaplain will take you and Miss Jewel home. You are an essential part of the foreseeable future, giving the nurture and assurance to a little girl, and her father, who wonders what happened to her mother. The chaplain will stay with you for a while if you like." In just a few more minutes Oroville Avenue traffic was flowing freely, as though nothing terrible had happened there.

Before they got out of the business district, the chaplain stopped at an Arby's drive-through and ordered half a dozen sandwiches. He explained, "A crisis often clarifies our priorities. Food is not important right now. You will need something to offer to Bruce, but you can get along for several days on granola and beef sandwiches. I'll make sure you don't run out of either. It's a practical thing I can do." His warm smile was welcomed by Tina who was trying to find the new center in all this.

When Bruce arrived at home there were still tears in his eyes. Tina asked if he would care for a Shasta Amber and gladly he nodded. The chaplain agreed to join him. Tina thought to herself, "Well at least this feels normal."

She went upstairs to check on a little girl who had struggled to settle down for her nap. When Tina returned the chaplain shared the content of their conversation. "Tina, we've just been talking about the changes that will need to happen for Jewel. It will be difficult for you to give her the attention and care she has been receiving if you remain in the room over the garage. That's a long ways from her crib. There are three bedrooms upstairs as well as the guest room down here. Do you think it will be possible for you to move into one of the rooms upstairs, nearer Jewel's? There is a bathroom in the hall up there as well as one in the master suite. For privacy, Bruce could even move to the one over the garage if you would prefer."

"I had already thought about being closer to Jewel," she answered. "But Bruce doesn't need to move. I promise not to bother him." A tiny smile said she was trying to lift the heavy pall that was on the morning.

Both men appreciated her effort. The chaplain then added, "We're afraid that your academic process might be on hold for a while. Jewel needs full time attention. Even night classes might be difficult if he is on a mission." They both studied her eyes.

"That's another one I have already thought about," she said softly. "I came here to care for Clara and her baby. Being a student was only secondary. Now that is more urgent than ever. I'll talk with Mrs. Russell to see if there is an on-line course I can take. It really isn't an issue."

Bruce said in the same soft voice, "Your salary was based on being a nanny. I'd like to at least double that in light of these new responsibilities."

Tina whispered, "Pay me whatever you like, but I want Nick Akimov to get what Butte Meadows got, blown to hell." The chaplain glanced at her and then back at Bruce.

Golly, the following month went by in a blur. After the front door was painted a distinguished burgundy to cover the golden G, Tina was moved into the bedroom next to Jewel's. The Akimovs were questioned extensively and they swore they had no knowledge of their son's participation in a radical group. Mrs. Russell allowed her to be enrolled in both a Human Resources class and Accounting 101 on line. There were three more accounting classes if she wanted to take them later. The chaplain conducted a wonderful memorial service for Clara and her ashes were scattered at Point Cabrillo near Mendocino, where they had spent their honeymoon. It was one of Clara's happy places. Her folks, Jeff and Holly Windsor, came from Seattle to share in those precious moments. Bruce traded in both the repaired Crown Victoria and Fiesta for a slightly used Taurus and a slightly more used '94 Thunderbird. Both cars were registered in both Bruce and Tina's names. Warm June rolled into hot July and except for finding the burned shell of Nick Akimov's Honda, there was no discovery of the Guerra's activities.

A very warm August morning found Bruce coming to the breakfast table in a very grouchy mood. He was like a storm cloud. Tina asked, "Is there something I can do to ease the morning?"

He tried a smile that didn't quite make it saying, "It's my lame folks. I didn't hear a peep from them after my phone call informing them of Clara's..." He still had trouble saying the words. "Telling them about the tragedy," he said. "Now they want to come out and visit Jewel. Not us, or me and surely not you," he practically growled. "They have the idea of taking Jewel to Virginia for a while, so she can have a stable home. My dopey mom even had the lack of grace to suggest that Jewel might live with them until it is time for her to go to school." Tina realized how angry he was when she noticed two tears drift unattended down his cheeks. "She said maybe when I remarry Jewel would have a normal home again." He slumped in his chair saying quietly, "Damn it, like I don't have enough stuff to deal with. Those Japanese guys are very excited about their idea and here I am playing footsy with my mom."

She slid him a cup of strong coffee creamed just as he liked it followed by a cheesy bacon and egg burrito. Her policy for changing a mood is, feed it.

Bruce called his mom to explain that Jewel was under doctor's care. "The trauma of seeing her mother bleed to death has created terrible nightmares," he explained. "She wakes me up every night screaming. I'm sure that would be very unsettling for you and dad." That seemed to put an end to it.

Mrs. Russell made an offer to Tina that had come out of a faculty meeting. As a courtesy to Clara's memory four professors offered to allow Tina to read the texts and lectures if she would attend the tests in person. They would find undergraduate students who would babysit while Tina was taking the tests. It accomplished two achievements: she could expand the subjects available to her and she had contact with sitters who would appreciate a bit of gratuity.

Bruce heard from his mom again before Thanksgiving. Once again she called asking for Jewel to come to Virginia, "Bruce, as a busy father, how can you imagine she could have anything but a broken heart, living without a mother? We can give her a wholesome home. Please, for decency's sake, let us give her a natural family. Then you can get on with your life and meet someone new. If you are remarried we could bring her to visit to see if it would be acceptable to Jewel."

Once again Bruce wanted to speak unkindly to his mother. But once again he said softly, "You know her Asthma has gotten worse. She uses oxygen most of the time. At night she wears a CPAP or else she has a hacking cough. I'm afraid it would be a terrible imposition on you to deal with her maladies." Once again he felt that the subject was closed.

To be sure there were missions, leads, tasks, duties of his job that kept him more than busy; yet thoughts of his unkind mother were a constant irritation and distraction to Bruce. Finally in February when she said they were coming out to California to get their girl, Bruce was bold enough to tell his mother that it would be a waste of their effort. "Hell will freeze over before I let my daughter go across the street with you, let alone to Virginia." There was silence on the other end of the connection. "I am ready to place a restraining order on you both. It has been almost a year since Clara's death and you haven't come to share my grief or Jewel's and yet you consider yourselves an ideal home. My advice to you is stay safely in Virginia where you belong and buy a dog to keep. Quit fussing about my daughter." He hung up without saying "goodbye," a fact that would haunt her.

A few more weeks plodded by when Bruce said, "I believe I was told your birthday is April 4th. Is that right?" A happy smile was lighting his face for once.

"That is correct," Tina answered sweetly, "three days before Easter this year."

"You'll have to explain to me how the date of Easter wanders around so. Some years it is in March, and then again it might be in April. How does it make up its mind?" Tina wondered if Bruce was just trying to start a conversation or if there might be some point to this. Before she could say anything, he asked, "If this is an important birthday, would you like to celebrate it by not cooking for once? Can you arrange for a sitter Sunday evening? I don't think we will be very late."

She was excited about the evening all week. She tried on several of the dresses from Lacey and finally settled on a lavender one with purple accents. She was really cute.

That was a fact that Bruce complimented immediately. "You are quite lovely," he said warmly. "There are going to be gobs of men saying, 'How does that old codger manage to get such a good looking date?'"

"Is this a date?" she asked in a flirty voice. "I've never been on one before and please, no more old codger references. You are only eleven years older and in terrific shape."

Ignoring her compliment, he said, "It is a super important evening to be sure. I'll be interested how it turns out." He had that great smile and Tina wondered if she should be cautious.

When they were seated and the serving person asked if

she could get them something to drink, Bruce ordered a Mai Tai for Tina and a Sangria for himself. The young lady asked if she could see some I.D. Tina was happy to show hers and even received a "Happy Birthday." Then the lady turned her attention to Bruce and asked, "And yours, sir?"

Chuckling, he offered his I.D. saying, "You've already increased the gratuity. It's been a long time since I was carded." It was a great beginning to an evening. They clinked glasses and shared small talk, mostly focused on Jewel. Tina had several recent stories that made Bruce laugh softly, and proudly. Tina felt the effect of the adult drink, a warm fuzzy feeling. She was convinced that one was quite enough for this night. The food was served and enjoyed. When the last crumbs of the blueberry tort were gone her anxiety was peaking for she wondered if Bruce had some plan for the remainder of the evening.

Finally he said, "I've been thinking a lot about you. Do you think you can complete your degree in a couple years?"

Happily Tina answered, "If I continue at this rate I can finish it. I still haven't declared a major, but everything I have is solid."

"When that happens," (she was glad he didn't say 'if') "will you still be willing to care for Jewel?" His brown eyes held hers.

"Of course I will. Jewel is my primary commitment." Her face was serious and her gaze as direct.

"How about when she starts school, will you still be her nanny?"

"Of course. I promised Clara that I would take care of her," she paused considering the rest of that sentence, "and you. Her dying breath was concern for 'them.' I've never had a thought about anything else." Her eyes began to tear up just remembering that awful day and the wonderful woman.

Bruce nodded saying, "So, for the next fifteen or so years you are dialed in. Is that right?"

Tina sat up more straight and answered, "I've never put it quite like that but yes, that's precisely what I mean."

"What about a career or possible marriage" he asked. "Wouldn't you like to start your own family?"

As though she had anticipated the question, Tina brushed the air with her hand saying. "I will have plenty of time for that later."

"Good," he said leaning a little closer toward her, "Now I can tell you the reason for this evening, apart from our celebrating your birthday. The chaplain and I have had several conversations. Think what would happen to Jewel if something fatal should happen to me. She would be a toss-up orphan. As much as you care for her, and I know that is a lot, the court could give her care to a grandparent, or perhaps, just as likely a court approved foster situation. What would happen to my estate? Again that would be a toss-up for attorneys, but no guarantee that Jewel would receive even part of it. Do you see where I am going with this?" He moved even closer to her. "I'm thinking about Jewel's future, not yours, and I am trying to say that in the kindest way. Tina, I appreciate, admire, applaud and a whole bunch of other nice but non-romantic words, you. You are wonderful. I gave my whole heart to Clara and now Jewel inherits it. I don't want you to love me, at least not more than a brother or an uncle. I do want you to think about becoming my wife, however." She caught her breath. "I am not asking you to share my bed; in fact that idea appalls my memory of Clara. You would become Jewel's step mother, however, a legal binding relationship. I've already asked my attorney to modify our will." Now tears were on Tina's cheeks. "If the worst might happen to me, as my primary heir, you could give her guidance and support in a secure home. If nothing happens to me in fifteen years, God willing, we can part as business friends, knowing a slightly bazaar loop-hole in the law. You would receive at least half of our net worth and I'll be sure my will affirms that.

"I've had a couple months to think about this," he said softly. "You are getting it all in one chunk this evening. Remember, as you think about this, it's not my importance or yours. This idea is protection for Jewel. Who knew the ramifications of her mom's death? But now we all need to think in another dimension. Will you think about this, maybe call the chaplain and talk with him about it?" He reached his hand across the corner of the table and she clasped it gently.

Tina was thinking, "After all these years, it really is true. The part of the moon you can't see is pink, precious pink." After a long silence, she said, "I have imagined what a proposal would be like. This is not star-struck with violins playing. But your intense love for your daughter is even more compelling. Let me pray about this for a couple days. Even on first hearing, however, I can see and understand your logic for it and the good it might achieve, stability for Jewel and for me." They continued to hold the other's hand tenderly.

In the following three days she had four lengthy conversations with the chaplain. His wise understanding and counsel added to her assurance that it was surely unusual, but this was not an impossible idea. She talked with Barb for over an hour one evening and heard her conclusion, "If you understand the purpose of the marriage and it is not sinful, then follow your heart. I saw how willing you were to love Mason and Maddy. You must love Jewel just as much. That is so much more than many fine marriages have to build upon. I think you should say, 'I do!'"

On the 7th of June they applied for their marriage license at the Butte County Courthouse. When given the chance, Tina officially changed her name to Crystal Meyers. She still didn't want to be an insult to the Lord. On Sunday the 13th at 4 o'clock they were married in the base chapel with a simple but tender ceremony. The entire ATF squad and flight crew along with their wives were in attendance. They all understood the significance of the marriage and gave their whole-hearted blessing to it. Major Marsh had the cooks prepare a barbeque dinner to add to the festivities. Several of the wives gave Tina a warm embrace and promised to be of support if she ever felt the need. Their affirmation was sincere enough to almost make her forget that she was the youngest by far in the room.

Hours later back in their happy home, Bruce was enjoying a Shasta Amber when he asked, "Is this a good time to talk about our finances?" Tina, now Chris again, was still so floating on wonder that she answered, "It may help me get my feet back on the ground. Those folks were just wonderful. Yes, let's talk about reality."

"Good, I was thinking the same thing. First, however, let me apologize in advance if my thick head might from time to time accidently call you Clara. I hope you don't take it wrong. It's almost happened a few times this week. I think it is because I'm so relaxed with you. I certainly don't mean to offend you. O.K.?" His smile warmed her heart.

"I know. It's already happened a couple times and I took it as a compliment. You were with a dear friend and I hope to become one too. It will never be anything but a blessing. Speaking of names, I will try to get used to my new one. How about if you call me Chris instead of Crystal. I think that sounds more playful, don't you?"

"Yes I do and I'll try my best to get it right."

Playfully she said, "So, where shall we start?"

He took a good pull on the beer and began, "Clara pretty much took care of the bills. Our two salaries have taken care of all the debts including the house payment." He thought for a moment and added, "Her two life insurance policies are in savings and the check book has a balance of about sixty thousand." He took another pull on the beer and waited for her questions.

Her happy grin didn't fade as she said, "I have no debt at all."

He interrupted her asking, "How about student loans?"

"No debts at all," she chuckled. "In high school I worked for Lacey Tagawa, as you know. She was generous and I was frugal. My savings account is still about ten thousand dollars and I pay off my Master Card balance every month."

"Well you are a peach," he said with admiration. "Do you have any suggestions for making this house run more efficiently?"

She didn't hesitate, since he asked. "Is the house on a thirty year loan?" He nodded. "And how many years have you been here?"

"Nearly eight years, I think," came the curious answer.

"I'm pretty sure you could save a bunch of money with two changes," she said wisely. He raised his eyebrows urging her to continue. "Your large savings accounts are earning less than one percent and the seven-plus percent interest on your home loan is eating up more than half of your payment each month. I think if you take some of that savings money and pay off the home loan, then take the rest of the savings along with about forty thousand from checking and put all that into thirty year Treasuries that will guarantee you good interest you will be surprised how soon your bank balance will be ready for another investment or two. It will change the picture from expenditure to income."

"But Kiddo," a favorite name that was not individual, "won't I lose my tax benefit if I pay off the loan?"

"Well sure. You will lose a couple hundred dollars in credit but save thousands of dollars in having no payment. Remember, you are paying more each month in interest than you are on the principal. What is your house payment, sixteen or seventeen hundred dollars?"

Bruce shrugged, "More like nineteen fifty."

Chris asked, "Do you get a tax credit of over ten thousand dollars? I doubt it. But that's what paying off your home loan would net you each year and the Treasuries are guaranteed to earn at least two percent instead of nothing, which is another two thousand in growth. That would pretty much pay for taxes and insurance."

Her smiling husband held out his hand. When she placed hers in it, he said, "Let's go to the bank during lunch tomorrow. I only received a small raise this year: I need to get you on the account. I think this is going to make a big difference."

Wednesday morning she was back at the bank making the transfer of funds to pay off the home loan. Wearing her bib overalls and a wide brimmed straw hat she felt like a happy homemaker. It went smoothly and she was just turning to leave when an elderly man entered the lobby. His gray hair was shabby and a scraggly gray beard covered his chin. She was about to look away but there was something about his stride that seemed familiar. She tipped her hat over her face a bit. The man did not have the stride of an old man. She pushed Jewel's stroller over to the side of the lobby and bent over as though adjusting the straps. It was his eyes! They were not the weary wet eyes of an old man either. O Lord, she recognized those eyes. She turned her face away so he was unable to recognize her, too. Carefully she made her way to the door and immediately outside, she called Bruce.

"Oh Lord, Bruce, he is here in the bank. Nick Akimov is in our bank." "No I don't think he saw me. He has gray hair and a beard, but I am sure it's him." She listened to instructions and then made her way across the street to the bus stop and took a seat. That only took a few more minutes.

"No, he hasn't come out yet." She listened again and asked, "How long will it take him to get here?" She scanned the busy street and buildings. "What am I looking for?" she asked in confusion. Then she looked up. Hovering at the end of the block was a small black drone. "Yes, I see it." "No he hasn't... There he is! He's going into the parking lot." She watched intensely, afraid that she might lose sight of him. "It's the green pickup." Obediently she looked down at her lap as though reading something. The green pickup turned at the corner and became part of busy street traffic. When she looked up the drone was gone as well. "Bruce, do you see him?" "Bruce?" He was no longer on the line. Instead, he and a spotter were in the Cobra hurrying to play switch surveillance on the pickup which was southbound on old highway 99.

They used a long-range lens as they circled at a safe distance but still able to maintain contact while the pickup made two more brief stops. Finally it turned off 99 toward Biggs. An ordinary looking rundown farm was soon its final destination. The driver got out to open a barn door. Now that the location was identified, an FBI surveillance team would find an observation base nearby to monitor the house closely. It was a good day.

June turned into an exceptionally hot July. It seemed to Chrissy that it was much windier than previous years. Maybe the hardest to ignore were the very noisy thunder storms that rumbled from the evening into the night. One after another the flashes and then loud rolling claps of thunder bombarded them; there was no way a nearly three year old could get to sleep.

"Chrissy, sleep with me?" she whined.

"Honey, your bed is too little for both of us," the answer whispered. Boom! Another clap of thunder made the child flinch.

"I sleep in the big bed with Chrissy?" It was the beginning of growing communication and longer sentences.

"If you potty in your big girl panties we'll move you back into your own bed. O.K.?" It was also a time of negotiation and incentive for Jewel to learn simple lessons in behavior. And golly, did she ever learn to talk about it! She was becoming a jabber-box. She loved stories about butterflies, birds, kitties that were happy and the wasp nest under the eve of the house became a scary villain. On her fourth birthday Chrissy introduced the eager listener to the Berenstain Bears.

In spite of Chris's charming attempts at cheerfulness, her creative ways to please Bruce and Jewel, there was a constant warning cloud in her attention. She was perpetually aware that Nick Akimov, the assassin, was in a farmhouse just a few miles away. September had another full schedule of off-campus sessions and by the time she was getting the house decorated for Christmas; Chris had 12 more credits toward graduation. Bruce had two very informative conversations with the Japanese travel promoter.

On Christmas day the FBI sent out an alert to all law enforcement agencies. The Biggs house, which had been very quiet for seven months, had a sudden influx of activity with an arrival of twelve or thirteen men. If this was the group known as the Guerra's, they were in a compromised situation and the SWAT teams of both the FBI and California Highway Patrol were moving into position. All other teams should be on alert as backup.

It must have been a shock for those in the house to see the convoy of power form a blocking position across the only road out. A loudspeaker hailed the house and ordered all occupants to come out with hands in the air. Just as it had happened in Marysville, an upstairs window was broken and a rifle shot struck the side of the SWAT vehicle. Immediately from the roof shield of the black war wagon a marksman fired back with a 308. sniper's rifle. One shot, one kill! Two figures ran from the back of the house to the barn. Moments later the green pickup crashed through the barn door, apparently trying to turn and run cross country. The first shot hit the driver's side windshield and the car slowed. The second shot hit the passenger side windshield. Two shots, two kills. Soren and Nick Akimov didn't even see the shooter who ended their lives. Justice had happened and there was no one to acknowledge it.

Seventeen men, three women and three children came out of the house with their hands raised. Two buses joined the formation to transport the handcuffed crowd who had their rights read to them and had heard the charges that might represent the rest of their lives in prison. Except for the three desperate casualties, the end of the Guerra's was uneventful, a job well done. At least that was what the law enforcement folks hoped.

"O.K." Bruce's playfully gruff voice conceded, "if you want to call it a date, I guess it is. But we are just having dinner at Cassidy's Steak House and then the drama department's play Man of La Mancha."

Playfully Chrissy tossed her curly hair in victory. "That sure sounds like a date to me." When they heard the actor playing the part of Don Quixote sing, "To dream the impossible dream," it felt like a wonderful date, too. All the way home they talked about the quality and the symbolic meaning of the play.

Perhaps it was the absence of the threat of Guerra's that introduced a fresh era of growth. It is true that time heals all wounds, or perhaps it was the attendance at the University Presbyterian church with two other ATF families. Chris could not recall a more enjoyable or productive time. Bruce had suggested they begin some family traditions, like visiting a new Zoo every New Year's Day.

He also shared with her the nature of the Japanese proposal. "They want to find someone to act as a golf agent for them," he said carefully. "The idea is they have a bunch of requests for a four or five day trip to U.S. golf courses. They need someone to make arrangements at top end lodging and tee times. They're trying to convince me that there would be a steady flow of three or four dozen every week. They suggested that the money would be much more than I am making now. I told them if they throw in a Bell Cobra I'd be interested." It would be the last time he brought it up, but she thought about it a lot.

They flew to Seattle to spend Easter with Jeff and Holly, Jewel's grandparents. That gave them the opportunity to visit another big zoo. In June they took advantage of the family time scheduled at the base pool. Jewel learned to paddle on the foam floaters and finally to swim by herself. It was a time of luxurious peace. By Jewel's fifth birthday she began preschool at the Presbyterian Church and Chrissy had enough credits to begin her MBA courses.

The new school year was just getting a grand start when the Butte County traffic helicopter pilot called in an unusual object on the top of the university administration building. Authorities, including ATF were requested to investigate.

A Chico police cruiser happened to be parked in front of the building at the time. The officers scrambled up the four flights of stairs to the roof access. What they discovered was Dr. Grigori Akimov pulling a canvas tarp off of a steel box about the size of a piano. In his hand was some sort of weapon. "You are too late!" he shouted as he pointed it at the officers.

Both men instantly drew their sidearm and fired, at least three rounds each. The assailant was dead before his body hit the roof. When they rushed over to remove the weapon from his hand they realized he had told the truth. The weapon was nothing more than a remote clicker that had activated a trigger on the metal box. They were too late to stop it. A lighted display on the side of the object was counting the seconds down from four hours. He must have planned to be safely away when the bomb went off.

A crowd of law enforcement people gathered within a couple minutes and became aware of the dilemma. The object, which had been fashioned from metal plates welded together, was about four feet by four feet with six large spray nozzles sticking out the top. Its weight had to be well over three hundred pounds. Under the tarp they found empty boxes that indicated C4 explosives and several empty containers that had "Phosgene" and "Chlorine" symbols. It appeared to be a primitive airborne gas bomb. There seemed to be no way to open the device to disarm it and it was too large and heavy to fit through a door. Someone suggested a mobile crane. Just as quickly someone else noted that even if they could get it off the roof it would still rain death and destruction on a mile radius of the school.

Major Marsh pondered, "If we could remove a couple of these radio antennas, we'd have enough clearance to move it with the Bell Cobra and dump it in the woods."

Someone else asked, "Could you get it to the ocean in four hours?" They all glanced at the display realizing that eight minutes more had slid away.

While Bruce was going through the warm up procedure, Perry Wilson, the co-pilot was removing the hinge pins to the port side door and the front two seats. There would be ample room to move the dangerous cargo.

Startled students looked up as the helicopter descended to less than a hundred feet over the quad and slid gently over the side of the administration building. It rotated to more easily address the steel box, and set down like a feather. Bruce advised the men who were going to lift the bomb to first place the tarp on the floor of the chopper. "That way it will slide right out when we roll to eject it." He also instructed officer Wilson to stand down. The advantage of two hundred pounds less would give him better speed and fuel mileage. It had taken only an hour and sixteen minutes to get the bomb off the roof.

"Chico One this is Cobra Seven, outbound west to the coast, over"

Cobra Seven this is Chico One. Roger the mission, out."

Thirty eight minutes later base heard: "Chico One this is Cobra Seven just crossing over the coastline, Over."

"Cobra Seven this is Chico One prepare to eject cargo in fifteen minutes. Over"

"Chico One this is Cobra Seven, roger fifteen minutes."

Fifteen minutes later, one minute after the false display had triggered the detonation of a tremendous explosion, one that instantly shattered Cobra Seven into a debris field, "Cobra Seven this is Chico One. Eject the cargo, over." There was no reply. "Cobra Seven this is Chico One. Eject the cargo, over." There was no answer. "Cobra Seven this is Chico One, over." There was no answer. "Cobra Seven this is Chico One, over." There was no answer. Only a few dead sea birds who had eagerly explored the debris for edibles marked the spot where Cobra Seven rested.

The news circulated across campus like wildfire. "A bomb has been removed from the administration building, saving us from being poisoned. Dr. Akimov was shot by the police and his wife was found dead from some sort of overdose." Officials would discover among his personal items that Dr. Akimov was the instigator and leader of the group known as "Guerra". It was too unbelievable to grasp. Isolated at home with her responsibility of tending to Jewel, Chris was oblivious to the shocking events of the day and the second wave of grief approaching.

She could not imagine what both Major Marsh and the chaplain were doing at her door. When she noticed their tight lipped somber faces however, she understood in an instant. Something horrible had happened. As she opened the door her eyes were closed as she was shaking her head.

The chaplain embraced her and whispered, "It was terrible, Chrissy. Bruce was on a desperate mission of mercy, which saved the school and perhaps the whole city. The bomb, which Dr. Akimov made, exploded just before Bruce could safely dump it in the ocean. I'm sure he didn't know when it happened." She was trembling with shock. "When we planned for the worst that could happen we had no idea it actually would. You're going to need courage to help Jewel through this. Are you strong enough?" He looked at her fondly.

Tears were flowing freely as her soft voice responded, "Jewel needs me to be strong, so I will be. I'm also thinking this would be a perfect time to go back up to Seattle. Her grandparents would be a welcome shoulder to cry on for us both. They are the only family we know. Are you sure that Bruce is gone? Might there be some mistake"?

The chaplain shook his head saying, "We thought there were four hours on the trigger. There were only two, which was enough time for him to get it over the ocean, where it apparently detonated."

Another sob shook her body. "I think Grandma Holly will be the practical help for us both right now." Her voice broke as she wept aloud.

Now the Major added, "There is an emergency furlough fund that we haven't used for a long while. Chaplain White, will you see to tickets as soon as possible?"

"I'll get right on that, sir," the chaplain said, grateful to do any positive task in such a heartbreaking moment. Embracing Chrissy once again, he said, "Pack a couple bags and be ready in a few minutes. I'm pretty sure there is a flight out before supper. We use it often."

While Chris waited for the chaplain, she wept and absently jotted:

"Eclipse of the moon, I've been told,
is when a shadow dark and cold,
Hides all its beauty and snuffs out its light.
I can't see its promise or guidance, try as I might.
What will I do without my moon, without my hope?
I'll do my best, holding her dearly, even as I grope.

When the eclipse is done and the moon is back to stay,
We'll bask in the new warm light; we'll find a new day.

The doorbell rang making Chris jump with surprise. When she opened the door a very sad Officer Wilson and his wife Sue offered words of condolence and a potted pink Gerber Daisy. "We are so sorry right along with you, Chris," Perry said softly."I was scheduled to be his co-pilot. At the last minute he told me to stand down to lighten the load. I think he knew how dangerous the mission was going to be. He saved my life." Tears ran freely down both faces.

Sue embraced Chris warmly saying, "If there is anything we can do to help you through this please remember that I want to be with you. This is more tragedy than any heart can handle. Please let me help you." Her blue eyes were searching the face of an overwhelmed young woman. "Please?"

Perry said quietly, "He's been talking to me about a Japanese deal. He had me convinced that ATF is not the sort of life that can raise kids or build good marriages. I guess now it's time to forget that and think about our job." He gave Chris a long hug. "Please let us know what we can do to support you." He offered her a business card. "Now there is no excuse. If you need anything give us a call." He was still weeping.

When Jewel asked again why Chrissy was crying, she was told, "Daddy was on a dangerous trip in his helicopter. He had to go way out over the ocean and he hasn't come back. While we are waiting for him to come home we're going to see Grandma Holly for a few days." The agony of not knowing was painful to them both. They hadn't said "Goodbye". They had nothing to hold. She thought it best to try to cushion the terrible news knowing full well there is no way to lessen the grief of it.

In the airport waiting room there were only seven others going to Seattle, a serviceman in tan camos, two young couples and two businessmen. Chris was seated close enough to the business men to hear the name Meyers repeated several times. Because they were speaking Japanese she couldn't follow their remarks, but she was trying. "What would the possibilities be?" she asked herself.

Recalling Japanese phrases from Mason, she asked, "Excuse me please, are you talking Mr. Meyers?"

The one seated farthest from her smiled and said in English, "We might communicate better speaking in your language. Yes, we have tried twice to find Mr. Bruce Meyers in his office. We had several other meetings planned and hoped that we could catch him. We are returning to our office in Kyoto with unfinished business here. Unfortunately our efforts have not been successful." He took a deep breath, obviously searching for the correct words. "Mr. Meyers seemed our best opportunity."

"I am his heir," she said with a catch in her throat. "Today Mr. Meyers failed to return to the base from a very dangerous mission. We are afraid he is no longer alive." The man had a shocked expression and there was a rapid exchange between the businessmen. "This is his daughter whom I am taking to her grandparents in Seattle. I am very sorry for your frustration. I am aware of your golfing plans and spoke just moments ago with another ATF officer who is very interested in seeing it developed here."

The man's sad face changed to a more hopeful smile. Now he said more lightly, "If we had met you a week ago we would have saved several hundred dollars and hours of frustration. I am very sorry if your fears come true. We never had the privilege of meeting Mr. Bruce."

"There are many 'ifs' in destiny," Chris said softly. "Perhaps the future will smile on this chance meeting. If you will give me a business card, I will contact you within the week to set up a planning meeting here in Chico. I will catch my breath and Officer Wilson will be with us then. I'm sure we can create a working model by spring." In the presence of such an enormous storm cloud of sorrow, this was an unplanned ray of hope.

As he offered his card, the man introduced himself. "I am Edward Sagimoto and this man who is about to hear happy news is my funder, Richard Otomori. For ease of conversation, many Americans are more comfortable calling me Mr. Edward and my secretary Mr. Lee. We look forward to our next conversation. In the meantime our prayers for your peace will be made in the temple. We admire your bravery in such a sad moment." It was time to board their flight to Seattle.

Two name changes happened while they were receiving the tender care of the Seattle grandparents. Holly was the first to begin using the name "Julie" for a precious little girl. And that little girl began calling Chris "Mommy."

The nurturing of their hospitality helped stabilize two survivors. While Chris may not have had the devotion of being his bride, there had been a wonderful commitment of affection for Bruce. As a daughter, Julie idolized her daddy and was coming to the realization that if he hadn't come home by now he must be with momma. She was sad whenever she thought about it. Yet ever so slowly and certainly she began to realize there was comfort when Chrissy said that she could pray with them any time she needed to talk with her Momma or Daddy.

Before they returned to Chico, Holly was trying to make holiday plans. "I know it is months away, but would you accept an invitation to have Thanksgiving with us? We will come to Chico if you don't want to travel. We just want to share it with you." Her happy smile underscored the pleasure of being together.

"We'll be happy to be here again," Chris replied. "I would love to be able to share in the dinner. How about Christmas? Would you like to enjoy a warm winter holiday? I'm sure it wouldn't be white."

Holly's smile faded a bit as she said, "We've already told our son Carter that we would spend Christmas with them in San Diego. He's in the Marine Corps doing data processing. We haven't seen much of him with his previous deployments in the middle east. But since Clara's death he is back in the states knowing that we don't want to spend the holiday alone." Her smile returned as she had an idea. "Let me call him to see if we can fit in two more. I'll bet you would like to meet the rest of the family and I know they are eager to meet you. We could stay at the Embassy Suites downtown, and you know, the San Diego Zoo is world famous."

When Julie heard the new plans, she was delighted to know that she had an aunt and uncle and two cousins. When she heard that there was another zoo to visit, she said quietly, "It's good that we are keeping daddy's plans going. He really likes the monkeys. I hope we can see them for him."

Chris gave the gentle five year old a soft embrace, realizing that she was trying in her own way to process the concept that her daddy wouldn't be coming home again.

A smiling Chaplain White greeted them upon their return to Chico Municipal, saying, "Welcome home, ladies. How are you holding up?" When Chris assured him that they were both coping, he added, "We've missed your smiling faces." He was guiding them toward his car. "Are you eager to get back to school" He was trying to be buoyant when he was sure there would be a host of grief reminders.

"I've had a couple phone conferences with Mrs. Russell, the registrar," Chris said gently. "She agreed that taking a break until next year might be a good plan. She understood that I must give first attention to Julie." Her face broke into a warm smile as she added, "I've also fanned the coals of an idea Bruce was working on. It might be a very big success." Even though he waited for her to continue, she didn't say any more. It would be better to see what the next month or so might bring.

Julie helped clear the dishes from the table then excused herself to her room where the Lion King video was waiting. She was so quickly becoming a young lady.

Mr. Edward eased back from the table exclaiming, "Miss Crystal, that was a most satisfying dinner. You cooked the lemon salmon outside on an open flame?" His smile was cheery.

"Yes, it is a gas barbecue. I like its convenience and the fish odor stays outside." This second planning meeting was even better than the first. Chris had asked Perry and Sue Wilson to join them. Their interest was exciting evidence that this was a great concept.

Mr. Lee, the secretary for Mr. Edward, commented, "Did you call the berries 'Black Berries'?" They are new to me but so very tasty. Thank you for a memorable dinner."

"You are very welcome in our home" Chris answered graciously. "Tonight I would like to confirm your plan and hear a report from Mr. Perry who has contacted hotels and golf courses near Los Angeles. Mrs. Sue, will tell you about the Palm Springs area and I will do the same for those near San Francisco."

Perry smiled as he said "This is a super exciting idea. You were right," he said looking fondly at Chris. "Those managers were very interested in hearing more about guaranteed business. We didn't get anything signed, but verbally there was at least a ten percent reduction in both green fees and hotel stays. You asked about Pebble Beach, but it is not open to the public and has about a one year reservation list for pros."

Sue added, "I checked on the hotels and courses in the Palm Springs area. Hotels are not as large there but each manager I asked assured me that they would welcome guaranteed lodging on Sunday through Thursdays. They would also give an additional ten percent reduction if the room was shared." Perry nodded agreement with that. "I thought the courses were more playable than those near the ocean," she continued, "there are less trees and water hazards." She smiled in satisfaction for a positive report.

Chris joined in that smile and said, "I also found most of the managers quite welcoming. There are over four hundred hotels in San Francisco. I'm sure there are many cheaper ones, I just contacted six of the top ten. They felt it was a very acceptable idea. I also talked to the folks at Shuttle Express to get them to the golf courses and back. The manager I spoke with said they could provide ten coupons at a reduced rate for each golfer. They would run a shuttle every fifteen minutes on the days the group was there. That seemed both timely and convenient. I also talked to a manager of a large golf equipment chain. Finding a sufficient quantity of rental clubs would be challenging, but highly welcome if we can guarantee numbers."

"The only challenge I foresee in this concept, "she continued quietly, "is that this offering is by groups not individuals. If they want to pick and choose their lodging and individual course, they will not receive the rates we are quoting. For a standard four day five night golf discovery a price of $4000 plus airfare, might seem excessive to some and a bargain to others."

"Are you adding a surcharge onto that for your service?" Mr. Edward asked.

"No sir," Chris said with a positive tilt of her head. "Those would be the advertised room and green fee rates. Our funds would simply be generated by the reduced group consideration. For this to work for us, there must be volume, groups of seventy golfers, eighteen foursomes. We could accommodate up to 280 before spilling to other hotels and courses. I have no idea where you see this maxing out."

While Mr. Edward asked questions about hotels and courses in the Los Angeles area, Chris served coffee and Angel Food cake with strawberry cream topping. Finally Mr. Edward and Mr. Lee had to retire to their hotel for the night, saying they had an early morning flight back to Kyoto. There was lingering enthusiasm for the concept and appreciation for their effort that had proved its sound possibility.

When they were gone, Perry asked Chris in a voice that sounded like a cub scout at a marshmallow roast, "Chris, do you actually think this could possibly happen?" Before she could answer he waved his note paper. "If we just had one full group a week that would be twenty eight thousand dollars! Multiplied four times that's a hundred twelve thousand a month and a million three forty four in one year!"

Chris shrugged and said, "It is possible and I'm pretty sure that is the slim end. You could work at home or I could finish my master's in my spare time. For sure it is something to think about. It wouldn't be bad if we only did one a week split between us. I could live with that!" Sue was nodding her agreement. "I just hope we are getting the whole picture from Mr. Edward," Chris said softly. "He's the only one who understands the scope of potential here."

As Sue was helping clean up the kitchen the ladies chatted about this big house. "Perry and I have been renting near the base for the past three years. We thought this might be a brief posting, so we've been undecided about making Chico a career. It's scary how fast a wishy-washy year can go by. We've got little to show for our time here."

Chris nodded in understanding. "I know what you mean, and just the opposite is also true. I've been so focused on school and Julie that five years have just been a blink. I promised Bruce that I would stay here until she goes to college. Now this big barn seems more burden than blessing."

Her friend asked, "How big is this house? From the street it just seems like a sweet stately home."

With a bit of a humorous tone, Chris said, "Stately, yes. I think Bruce and Clara were planning to fill it with a large family. There are four bedrooms upstairs, the guest bedroom down here and a basement that was remodeled to be a two bedroom apartment with a full bathroom. Of course there is also the apartment over the garage. I'm not sure how sweet that all is."

"It sounds pretty sweet to me," Sue said with a grin. "Ours is a two bedroom one bathroom that hasn't a chance at hosting folks for a visit".

"If you ever want to have family visit." Chris was still caught up in "Let's make a Deal," "there would be surplus room here." She was thinking in a problem solving mode. "They could stay here. We would welcome new friends." The evening concluded with some spirited speculation of what might develop from the meeting with Mr. Edward.

Just after nine the next morning, Sue called asking, "Good morning, friend. What do you girls have planned for today?"

"Well, I just dropped Julie off at Preschool. I'll pick her up at noon and we'll probably have peanut butter sandwiches for lunch, unless we get a better offer." She snickered at her own boldness.

Sue's voice was a bit more excited, "How about meeting us at the Burger Barrel? We came up with a fun idea last night." She didn't say any more. That was probably enough to arouse Chris's interest. "See you at about 12:15?"

When the sandwiches and milkshakes were served, Julie bowed her head for a moment. When Perry and Sue looked at Chris expecting a grace, she shook her head. "She says a silent prayer of thanks to her folks for providing such a good lunch. She prays at every meal." A tear ran down Perry's cheek.

He took a deep breath and said, "Our lease is ready for renewal. We're wondering if there might be a way for us to rent the garage apartment from you. We could finally save some money for a down payment on our own place and you would have someone around to help in the kitchen or house chores. I am pretty handy." His smile was now a confirmation of good will.

Sue added quickly, "Would a thousand dollars be about

half of your mortgage payment? That would save us about five hundred dollars a month. We could share cooking chores and expenses. Don't you think that would be helpful?"

Chris's warm smile was caused by the realization that these friends were trying to make it sound like they were being blessed by a suggestion which was one hundred percent intent on providing Julie and her security and comfort. What amazing friends. Chris went along with the notion. "If you took the downstairs guest bedroom we could share the house and have the garage and basement apartments for your visiting family. I've been thinking about how nice the basement would also be for an office as well. If we get the golfers going, that could be real useful and so convenient."

Chris received a very unusual phone call from Mrs. Russell. "Chris I know it is late for business calls so I'll try to be brief. The Alumni newsletter is called the Chico Log. I have had a request from Dr. Roseman for some guest contributors to write a brief article for the Blog portion. He is aware of your consistent high quality papers. Do you think you could write something for the November issue, something about gratitude?"

Chris smiled before she answered. It was strange for she had recently been aware how blessed she had been even with all the grief. "I believe that would be a welcomed assignment," she answered brightly. "You did say brief didn't you?"

"Thank you for considering it," the registrar fairly sang. "Most of the folks I ask are too pressed for time to do gratis assignments. If you will keep it to one page single spaced we can fit it in the November issue. Thank you, sweet lady, for your inspiring attitude. My job is not always pleasant. When I speak with you however, I know my soul will be lifted. I'm already eager to read your offering. Thank you."

Chris opened a fresh document and wrote: "I just read a copy of a letter printed in the World News Magazine. It seemed to me to sum up much of what is best about this beloved land of ours. It demonstrates the Thanksgiving spirit and our American character – not only for ourselves but millions of less fortunate around the globe. The letter is written by Radarman first class Jerry Richards aboard the aircraft carrier *Midway* on station in the troubled waters of the South China Sea.

"Dear Mom and Dad," he wrote.

"Today we spotted a boat several miles off any land and we rendered assistance. We picked up 65 Vietnamese refugees. It took about two hours to get them all aboard, and then they had to be screened by intelligence, checked out by medical, and fed and clothed. Now they are resting on the hanger deck and not one is complaining about the accommodations. They are just grateful to be off that sinking ship. There are several kids sitting in front of probably the first television set they've ever seen – watching 'I Dream of Genie.' They had been at sea for five days and were out of food and water. All in all a couple more days and that crowd would have been in serious trouble.

"I guess once in a while, we need a jolt like this for us to realize why what we do is so important. I mean, it took a lot of guts for those parents to make a choice like that – to go to sea in a leaky old boat in hopes of being found by someone who would rescue them. So much risk! They must have felt it was worth taking such a big chance rather than live in hopeless oppression. For all our problems with the price of gas and not being able to afford a new nicer place to live, I really don't see any leaky old boats heading out of San Diego, looking for a Chinese or Russian ship to give them aid.

"I'll never forget the scene as we approached them. They were all waving and as best they could, trying to say, 'Hello, American sailor, hello freedom man'! I guess it can't be said much clearer than that. America has always been a place a man or woman can come for freedom. I know we are crowded and we have unemployment and bad traffic, but I pray we will always find room to help. We have a unique society made up of castoffs of all the world's wars and oppressions and yet we are strong and free. We have one thing in common. No matter where our forefathers came from, we believe in that freedom. I hope we will always have room for one more person who doesn't have to worry about their family starving or an ominous knock on the door at night; where all women and men who truly seek freedom and honor and respect and dignity for themselves and their posterity can find a place where they can finally see their dreams come true. Who knows; perhaps in that huddle of wet refugees we may have just saved a doctor, a teacher, a contractor, a soldier or a sailor. I hope so.

"Love, Jerry"

As I read this letter I became aware that we Americans are still uniquely blessed – not only with the rich bounty of our land, but a bounty of the spirit which pauses to gather together and give grateful thanks for being numbered among those who count our greatest gift the birthright of being an American. Happy Thanksgiving! Until we meet again, be your own BFF. Submitted by Chris Meyers"

By the time Chris and Julie left to spend Thanksgiving in Seattle the pieces had all fit together. The Wilsons were living in this wonderful shared residence. Sue showed her organizational competence by managing the first two waves of golfers. She received one payment from Mr. Edward for the entire group. She then made lists of the names for the hotel and golf courses; transferred payments to each and ordered shuttle coupons. Because of a more favorable weather opportunity, they were sent to Palm Springs. The first group went to the Desert Riviera and the second to Del Marcos Hotel. It worked perfectly and raving approval insured an even more rapid growth. Mr. Edward had agreed that an interpreter would be a practical addition. Mr. Lee accompanied the group and was added to the golfing list. It turned out to be a sweet job for him. The trio agreed that "Western Promotions" was good for a business license name for their enterprise and Chris suggested that this phenomenal income might be changed into Treasuries, since it was not needed for day to day support. Perry decided to stay with ATF for the foreseeable future and Chris signed up for her Master's program.

Perhaps the most important change at the time was the tender moment of prayer before every meal. Perry held Sue's hand and thanked God for the unexpected blessings and renewed strength from this food. He asked that God might reveal in his mysterious way what we might do to advance his Kingdom, to bring heaven a bit closer on earth. Even little Julie bowed, not sure what the words meant. Her sweet voice always joined in the "amen" because she did grasp the meaning of that.

"I'm telling you the truth," Chris's smile tried to convey her sincerity. "We are going to San Diego to meet Clara's brother and family. I'm not just trying to get out of the way. Your folks will be comfortable here and there is no need for them to be in a hotel."

Sue answered with a bit of embarrassment, "It will be the first time since our wedding that all the folks will be together. We never dreamed we could offer them all Christmas hospitality. Are you sure?" When once again Chris wrinkled her forehead as though she were becoming angry, Sue chuckled, "I'll make sure all the linens are fresh before and after their stay. Once again I am so blessed by you." She gave Chris a warm embrace. "We are so blessed!"

Chris sat on a beach blanket watching the waves breaking and rolling up the sandy shore. Carter had been cordial but obviously uncomfortable around her. She was a reminder of Clara's death, so he was taking a walk. Now as Jeff and Holly strolled down the beach and the children played on some nearby swings, Carter's wife, Cindy, was trying to build a new bridge by asking questions.

"You were hired to be a nanny?" she asked.

"I was," Chris cheerfully answered. "Our agreement was that I could help Clara the last three months of her pregnancy. Then as she was able, I would stay with Julie when Clara went back to teaching. Any classes I could take here and there were ideal." She studied the eyes of a woman who was trying to overcome some feelings of sorrow, with perhaps a bit of angry suspicion.

"Were you with Clara when it happened?" The words were barely audible.

"She was driving and I was beside her," Chris spoke with a very soft whisper. "Julie was in the car seat in the back. It was so horrible; the bullet hit her throat."

"I can imagine. I was told she bled to death. Is that right?"

Chris nodded then softly said," A second bullet went through her chest." There was a long silence with only the rumble of the waves and the call of sea birds.

"And Bruce proposed to you a year after it happened?" Cindy asked. Her eyes searched Chris's.

"A bit more than that, I think. It was such a bad time." Chris was not prepared for the next question.

"Were you sleeping together then?" The words were spoken quietly but the painful shock made Chris flinch. Tears formed in her eyes and she got up and walked away.

Cindy ran after her trying to get her attention. "Wait! Chris, wait!"

She was nearly to the car before Chris turned and said, "I came here because your mother-in-law invited me." The words were clipped and full of emotion. "Carter has avoided me and now you insult the hell out of me. Bruce would have called this a cluster mess" She took a ragged breath and said, "Obviously you have little of Clara's heart." Before Cindy could say a word of apology, Chris continued. "I am a twenty five year old virgin. That is nothing to be proud of or ashamed about. I was married to a wonderful man who made it very clear that the only bed he ever wanted is Clara's; anything else was appalling to him. That is something to treasure. Our marriage was a safeguard for his daughter, in the event he might lose his life and she would have to live with someone who can only think ugly twisted thoughts, as you do. I am disgusted at your shallowness and just plain sorry for you. Coming here was a terrible mistake!" She turned and walked to the car leaving a tearful woman to absorb those painful words.

Plans were to begin at Windsor's' for Christmas Eve dinner and then a service at their church. Chris made her apology to Holly saying, "Please forgive me for being worn out from the day. I'll stay here and get some rest. I'll be bright and shiny in the morning." She knew Julie was having a wonderful time getting to know her cousins.

On Christmas morning Julie was beside herself with energy. She opened three of the gifts Chris had brought for her. When Holly knocked on their door saying they were ready to go to brunch, Chris once again begged off saying that perhaps something had upset her stomach. She asked if she could just remain at the hotel and get some rest. Julie felt sorry for her because there was going to be a lot of good food and fun games to play.

A few minutes later the knock on her door was another of those startled surprises. She thought it might be someone from the hotel staff, instead she found Carter Windsor.

"Chris, may I apologize?" he asked quietly. "Cindy told me what she asked. There are no words adequate to undo the hurt. I will tell you that she does have a good heart." His smile grew. "She does lack any sort of social filter, however. It is her only trait that I don't adore. Her mouth is frequently in action before her brain is engaged, as they say. Please give us a second chance to welcome you into our lives. Mom has told us that sis died in your lap as you tried to stop the bleeding. You are like a saint to me." Now there was a tremble in his voice as he said, "Please forgive us." He held out his hand.

As she shook his hand she said, "I'll just switch into something a little more appropriate." It was her way of demonstrating that she was working on having a gracious heart like Clara's.

"You look just great," he said jubilantly. "Come on, they're waiting brunch for us."

While they were driving up the La Jolla hills, Carter asked her about school, her goals, finally he got around to her family.

She gave him the quick version. "My family imploded when I was just a little girl. Dad worked in some boatyard down here; mom wound up in jail. My older brother went into the Marines and my little brother was somewhere in a foster home. I completely lost track of everyone."

"What's your Marine brother's name? Maybe we've bumped into one another."

"I doubt that," she said quietly. "I think he went in ten or twelve years ago. He's probably out by now, but it would be good to try. Michael Gerald Winter is his name and I think he enlisted down here someplace in California."

"I'm an analyst in data processing so it will be easy to take a peek"

Carter pulled into the driveway of a Spanish style home with a red tile roof. "This is a lovely home," Chris said appreciatively. "Did we just pass the school that Lucas and Sarah attend?"

"Yes indeed," he answered. "He's a third grader and she's in the first grade. They think it is cool that they get to walk to school every day."

"Is Cindy employed outside the home?" she tried to sound interested.

"Yes," Carter answered brightly. "She's Customer Service for Global One, the cell phone people."

Chris nodded in understanding, choosing not to verbalize what was on her mind.

As they entered the Christmas adorned home, Holly and Julie hurried to her. Holly to hug her saying softly how glad she was that Chris was feeling better. Julie was eager to show her a lovely new doll.

"Look Mommy," she giggled, "her name is Mini-me. She has pigtails just like me. Isn't she just the cutest?"

Chris embraced her and answered, "Yes you are!"

A humble Cindy offered her hand in greeting saying, "Merry Christmas, Chris. Thank you for a second chance. I've been enlightened about your commitment to Julie and self sacrifice following Clara's death. I do apologize for my behavior. Will you forgive me and join us for a Mimosa?" The brunch was starting very well.

When the dishes were finally emptied and cleared and the children were busy with their new gifts, the adults exchanged wrapped presents. There was much of the polite, "Oh you shouldn't have" exclaimed when the men each opened a dozen golf balls and the ladies were given a $100 day spa certificate from Chris.

Holly said, "Chris that is so very generous of you."

She wanted to say more but Chris waved her off saying, "Bruce had an idea for a new career path. He had been talking with a couple travel agents from Japan who want to send golfers here. It is cheaper for them to fly over here and stay in a fine hotel rather than try to get on a golf course over there. In our first five week trial, we have generated four hundred thousand dollars. I think Bruce wants to share some of the bounty with you. Just wait until next Christmas." Her smile of satisfaction was radiant.

Jeff asked, "How many of you are involved? You used a plural 'we'."

"Bruce's co-pilot on that last mission was asked to stand down to lighten the load on the chopper. We are pretty sure

Bruce understood how dangerous his mission was and so saved Perry's life. Perry and Sue Wilson are in this new effort with me. They are also renting the downstairs guest room."

Cindy started to ask a question but Chris noticed Carter shake his head preventing it. He asked, "Will this new effort prevent you from continuing your studies?"

"Oh no," Chris beamed. "Julie gets first priority but she's in preschool from nine 'til noon. My Master's classes are on line except for tests and Sue is there to cover for me for those few times." She thought that would answer his question.

Carter asked for clarification, "But how much time do the golfers take?"

Chris's smile did not diminish, "That is Bruce's brilliance; it required only a few minutes for each wave of golfers. We get a list of names from the travel folks and a check to cover all their expenses. That list is forwarded to the hotel and selected golf courses along with a pre-agreed payment. We send them coupons for Shuttle Express so they can get to the hotels and then the concierge take over. So far it has worked smoothly to the satisfaction of golfers and agents alike."

With a sincere face, Jeff asked, "How much of a pipeline do you have? It seems like that would be a fairly short supply of golfers."

Chris made a pouty face saying, "I really don't know. Mr. Edward, our agent in Kyoto, says we are not keeping up with the demand there and who knows how many there might be in some of the larger cities when this catches on. We'll be booked months in advance."

Carter asked, "When you finish your MBA will you stay in Chico or would you consider living nearer cousins?"

She smiled warmly. "Thanks for saying 'when' and not 'if.' I think we will want to be near the family we have. Both cities are pretty expensive but I do believe Seattle is more friendly with a couple grandparents." She glanced at Cindy. "But we really love this zoo. We'll be here often." The remainder of the afternoon was basically small talk and the sound of happy children building memories.

"Good morning, Perry." Her voice was welcome to him. "I promised I would call you before we left." She listened and then replied, "Yes, Southwest 118. We stop for just a few minutes in Orange County and will arrive in Chico about 11:30. I'll get a cab for us." She listened. "No, it will not be a…" "O.K. if you are that eager to get out we will be happy to see you, too." Chris listened for a moment then replied, "She did great. Gram Holly gave her a CD player with a headset. She has two discs of Kipling's *Just So Stories*. Jack Nicholson narrates and Bobby McFerrin provides the jazz background." "Yeah, I know. She hasn't put it down long enough for me to listen." "Yeah, me too. We'll see you then."

She was about to hang up when Perry added, "Hey. An agent from NSA has called twice for you. He says we must produce some sort of file for all the Japanese we are bringing into the country. I tried to deflect him but he is pretty focused. He said he would be back this afternoon to see you."

Chris sighed softly, "Well, so much for rest and relaxation. We'll see you in a while. Weren't you the one that said we have more government than we can afford?" They shared a chuckle as they hung up.

It wasn't much of a drive from the municipal airport but Perry was trying to give her the report. "Mr. Edward told us there would be the regular seventy three. But he called back to say there had been a sudden clamor to be added. We had a request for 290! Sue called the downtown Holiday Inn; they are probably the largest. She was told they were anticipating a short demand week. They were happy to take them all. The manager told us that any group over two hundred gets a seven percent additional credit. Because of a mild weather forecast, Sue booked the golfers into the four San Mateo courses, which are convenient. Wow, did that work out neat! Our share for the week is about two hundred ten thousand dollars!" He looked at her directly. "For one week! And he thinks the new year will be just as vigorous."

Chris studied the grateful man and said, "Let's have an apple crisp for dessert tonight. We need a serious conversation about what direction we want this windfall to take us. It's time we get serious about our organizational structure and goals."

Chris was happy to be back in her kitchen. She had thawed a beef roast, then boiled it in beef broth for a couple hours until it was tender enough to pull apart with forks. Now it simmered in marinara sauce while she was baking yeast rolls. Spaghetti Squash and sautéed sliced mushrooms would make it a super dinner. The doorbell interrupted her satisfaction.

Two men flashed I.D. badges as she said, "I was warned some government guys would be around." With a short laugh, she tried to ease the introductions with humor. "You're not dressed well enough to be Mormons."

"Good afternoon Mrs. Meyers. I'm Gunnery Sergeant Charles Randall and this handsome man is my partner Dennis Burke. We are a Mobile Investigation Team of the NSA. May we have a few minutes of your time to clear up a question? We won't interrupt your meal preparation; it does smell delicious."

Perry stepped near the open door saying, "What's the deal here? Who are you guys actually? NSA doesn't have anything like a mobile investigation team. Are you bogus or part of a National Security Strike Team?" He was showing his ATF I.D. as well and it was obviously authentic.

"Well aren't you the snapdragon?" Mr. Randall snickered. "We are NSA pondering what you are doing bringing over five hundred Japanese men into the country in the past two months. We'd like to see some documentation." His expression had become more serious with Perry's insightful understanding.

Chris remained cheery, however, as she said, "Gentlemen, come on in. You obviously are confused about who you are with and what you are seeking. We are not information gatherers for any security agency. You're not even asking the correct folks. All these golfers came through security and customs following appropriate protocol. They are golf fanatics on a brief vacation, all legal and approved. If you are so curious you should be asking customs. Let me get you a Shasta Amber so it's not a complete waste of your time." As the men were being seated Sue was introduced and Julie came down from her room, but was eager to get back to hear the rest of her *Just So Story*.

After a couple refreshing sips, Mr. Randall asked, "So, tell me how this multi family thing works. How are you all here?"

Before Perry or Sue could answer, Chris said with a small snort, "Stars and little fishes, there you go again asking the wrong question." Mr. Randall gave her a startled glance. "Our living arrangement is none of your business either." The words could have been received as hostile. Her happy demeanor, however, kept it light. "The question you should ask is 'Who are we?' This is agent Perry Wilson of the Chico division of the ATF. Sue, his wife is our golfer's angel. She makes hotel and green fee arrangements for Kyoto travel agents. I am the widow of the ATF pilot that did not return from a bomb disposal mission in September. You must have heard about it. We are saluting him this evening by sharing his favorite beer. If there is any of that that alarms you or your agency, I suggest you contact our attorneys. This afternoon is far too pleasant to be distracted by fishing questions." She lifted her bottle in a toast and they followed her example, even if it was the first time she had ever tasted a beer.

"Gentlemen, if you would care to join us for supper, we have plenty and you can wash up just down the hall." She never lost her gracious charm and the agents were no longer concerned about Japanese golfers.

A couple satisfying hours later, Randall and Denny were on their way back to Sacramento. "Wasn't that uncanny?" Denny asked. "It was just like having the boss right there."

"I know! I about spit out my beer when she said 'Stars and little fishes.' How many times have you heard him say the same damned thing? But I think it was something about her eyes. She's younger than him, what do you think, four or five years?" Randall was obviously enjoying the moment. "When she squared up on me it was almost laughable. She shot me down but I liked it. Damn, that is one fine woman and what a cook besides!"

"I know!" Denny answered. "When she saluted her dead husband my heart nearly stopped. You don't find one like that very often." Both men nodded, reflecting on special moments they had shared with Chris.

Randall said softly, "I think I'm going to find several excuses to come to Chico in the near future."

The dishes were in the dishwasher and Julie was tucked in snugly, finally they could get down to the business part of the evening. Chris began, "I don't think any of us, Bruce included, had any idea how well this golf thing would work. How are you two feeling about it?"

Perry spoke first. "For me very little has changed. I get to go to work as before, except now I never worry about bills or budget. There is a surplus each month and I know we are not going to fuss about money. I just get to do my job."

Sue's smile bloomed widely as she added, "Before I worried about our budget too. That took the luster out of my day. But I also worried about spending my day alone, hoping there was no incident, worrying about what to fix for supper, worrying about when we could see our folks again. I just did a lot of fretting. Now I have you and Julie, this comfortable place and a growing bank account. It's all great."

"I'm also very content with the current situation," Chris

sighed. "I do suppose we should put some safeguards in, however. We are bound to be audited by IRS with this amount of money flowing through. Sue, if we set up a business account for Western Promotion, we can have two signatures, yours and mine. As CFO your duties could be receiving the payments from Mr. Edward. Each day will be unique, so you can give me an assigned sum for the hotel and green fees. That will be my job as treasurer to transfer payments to them and to us also, paying projected withholdings. I will divide our share into thirds two for you and one for me."

Perry started to argue with the cut saying it should be fifty-fifty, but Chris said that three individuals were involved and each should receive a share. "Let's try it for six months and see how we feel about it then. Changes can always be made later. We are just in the beginning phase of this. I'm content with this if you are," Chris said softly.

"It is unfair in our advantage," Sue protested. "I've been thinking Julie should get Bruce's share. Like you said, we can adjust it if we see it's too out of line." Perry agreed and Chris felt out-voted so they agreed to review the split in three months.

"One other thing I've been thinking about," Chris said with a twinkle in her eye, "is the question of when are you going to start your family? This would be a very opportune time with all this room and funds."

It was Sue's turn to chuckle an answer. "Funny you should mention that. We were talking about it while you were in San Diego. Don't you have about a year and a half to finish your Master's?" When Chris nodded with her head tipped at an interested angle, Sue asked, "Do you plan to remain here or will you want to be near family?"

Now Chris understood the direction of the discussion. "I told Carter we would probably want to be near Gram Holly. I remember once hearing the words of Mark Twain. He said, 'The mildest winter I ever had was the summer I spent in

Seattle.' We've had all the hot summers we need. I'm not sure but I suspect we will sell this place and move near Seattle."

"Well I can tell you," Sue spoke in a confidential whisper, "that we are already trying. We talked about it and request a first right of refusal when you sell. In a year and a half we will be able to top your best offer with cash."

"But what about Perry's dream of having his own helicopter instruction?" Chris felt it had been an expressed plan for the future.

With a girlish smile Sue said, "There is no rule against having it all, is there? Family first, then home, then flight instruction school." A bit more wistfully she added, "Just think what seventy five more weeks might generate. Why, I could retire." A giggle punctuated their conversation.

One afternoon Chris picked up Julie from preschool. The young child had a large question. "Mommy, how do I get a brother or sister? There is only one other girl in my class that doesn't have one. I would very much like a brother." Her curls bounced as she nodded her head and steady innocent eyes studied Chris closely.

"Well, Honey," Chris was not sure where this conversation might go, "there isn't a sister or brother store where we can get one. It takes a Mommy and a Daddy." She emphasized the word. "Together they get to have a baby, if they are very blessed." That seemed both honest and vague.

"How soon can you get a Daddy for me?" that delightful child wondered.

Chris knew that the subject was far too serious than to laugh so she tried to keep a straight face. "Julie Sweet, I've got about a year and a half of school that is taking all of my attention when I'm not with you. I just don't know how I would find you a Daddy." Curiously her memory replayed the light blue eyes of Charlie Randall and his happy smile. He had not over-reacted to her blunt words. Quickly she tried to erase the thought.

"Stars and little fishes, Mommy," Julie's sweet voice said softly, "I'll be too old to play with him then. I think you should lighten up about school and get with finding me a brother." She turned and watched the familiar street as they made their way home. Apparently she had voiced as much as she wanted to say about the matter.

Read the textbook, read the lecture, take the test. It was a rhythm of the winter, accompanied by the refrain, golfers, golfers, golfers.

But in south Texas a much more serious episode was playing out. The NSA Mobile Strike Team was taking an attack position around a suspected drug compound south of Carrizo Springs. One of the NSA officers had been accosted by a group of drug dealers. He did not survive the street brawl and they had no idea of the trouble that was slowly encircling their isolated hideout.

"Randall, take Denny around to the front gate. There is probably some sort of guard. Take him out. We'll go in through the kitchen. Let's make no more noise than is necessary." When they nodded compliance, he said "Remember, we are taking no prisoners. Let's do it for Dan." Four went toward the dark door while the other two were immediately only dark shadows moving toward the first casualty. In the following four minutes death was a swift judgment on fourteen men. Antonio Ruise, the leader in charge, was not one of them. In the kitchen cooler, however, they found a desk with a couple hundred plastic bags of white powder and beside it a stack of boxes filled with one hundred dollar bills, which verified the mission.

Randall asked, "Mike, what shall we do with all this?"

"Our instructions are to get rid of it," the squad leader answered the question everyone was thinking. "I do believe they don't really give a damn how that happens. I saw a gas can by the back door. Let's empty that on the smack. Set your incendiary grenades for fifteen minutes, two in here and at least six around the other rooms. We want this to be an inferno. What you don't want to carry home for our expenses will be turned into ashes." He paused to make sure the team was clear about the instructions. They began filling their field packs. Before they set their timers Michael opened all the propane knobs on the stove. They were well over a mile away when the night sky took on an orange glow. The fire would ignite the dry brush surrounding the compound and challenge whatever fire department might be available. There would be no lingering sign of the interdiction.

All the way back to Coronado Randall talked about the living wonder he had met in Chico. "No joke," he had said. "This lady is so different. She is fine to look at and stood up to me without a blink. I think she might be the one."

Michael chuckled, "Make up your mind; is she the smartest woman you've ever met or dumb enough to fall for your charm?" The team joined in laughter although they were all carrying heavy bags of bills.

Chris reread the lecture manuscript. The speaker was a department head from the Bureau of Corrections reporting that one of our government's major expenditures, 74 billion dollars annually for prison operations, is designed for failure. With 2.2 million incarcerated and an additional 4.7 million on probation or parole our prisons are at least 50% over populated. It costs our country $47 thousand dollars each year to house each prisoner; a rate growing three times faster than public education. The word "recidivism" was new to her. It means the rate those released from prison commit those crimes again. Over 50% are convicted again and if the crime involves drugs the number is more like 75%. The system is designed to get offenders in and keep them in, but it does not prepare them to stay out when their sentence is complete.

Yesterday's presentation was about identifying the fertile ground for success. The mantra was, "Find a need and fill it!" This information before her seemed like an enormous need calling for attention. There was already a movement toward privatized incarceration. Why didn't she have stock investment in that? It had already tripled in value in a year!

There must be a plan that is superior to what is already not working. She thought on it all evening and into the night. In the morning Chris was still pondering, "How can I invent a better wheel" She concluded that perhaps the table grace might be a place to ask for divine guidance.

Mrs. Russell called again seeking another blog article for the Log newsletter. "We've had such a positive response from the November issue we wonder if you could give us a suggestion on New Year's resolutions?"

"Ma'am, are you asking a student who has already been here seven years with at least one more to go for wisdom advice?" Chris chuckled .

"Chris, it is not your longevity we admire, it's the fact that you are on track for summa cum laude status. I think it was Oscar Wilde who said 'life is too important to be taken seriously.' If you will write your BFF theme, I'm sure we will all enjoy it in the January issue."

Be your own BFF:

"Have you noticed the deep lines and sagging faces of those who do not laugh enough? Resolution number one for 2007 is: first learn to laugh, especially at yourself, for that is the true definition of a sense of humor. While the unexamined life, according to Mr. Plato, is not worth living, life without laughter is not even worth examining.

"The second resolution is: believe deeply in your own

human fallibility and that you may be only 85 percent right on any issue. An aphorism says, 'What is the greatest gift of life" Wisdom. "And what is wisdom?" Good judgment. "How does one obtain good judgment?" From experience. "And how does one obtain experience?" From bad judgment!'

"The third resolution is to remember that our generation will live to be 115 years old. That means you will spend 85 years being over 30. Given that life span, you might keep in mind that the real tragedy of life is that loss of righteousness which fades inside a person while he or she is still living.

"Fourth resolution is be prepared to lose once in a while and search for ways to win again. I applaud the speaker who said, 'We have made a national fetish of success and victory. Failure is no disgrace. How do we know our own limits without failure? Those who try most will fail most.'

"Finally, if you have anything important to say in 2007, remember that one does not need to shout to be heard. A wise man once said, 'Strange how a soft voice can roar, and how a roar can seem inaudible." Most of all remember to laugh, for without laughter it will not be worth examining."

Be your own BFF! Chris Meyers

Sue answered, "Of course we will look after her. Perry is bringing pizza take-out. If you won't be here, he can just get one large half and half. Julie likes cheese pizza doesn't she?" When Chris agreed, Sue continued, "Did he give you a hint what his agenda might be? I can't imagine he is still nosing around the golfers."

"I really don't know," Chris answered with a grin. "We've had two long phone conversations that started talking about the golfers but turned out to be more social than business. He was sort of vague. Personally I get the feeling he just wants a dinner companion. But if he is willing to drive up from Sacramento just to chat, it might be an interesting evening."

She smiled warmly. "I have had very few social opportunities and welcome the invitation."

Sue laughed softly with her best friend. "At first I worried that he might want in on the golfers' deal, but now I think you're right. I'll bet he was really impressed with your first meeting. Now he wants to see if you are really that wonderful. Don't fall for his sales pitch." Again they shared a humorous moment.

When Sue answered the doorbell she was aware of Mr. Randall's promptness. That was a good sign. But when Chris joined them, wearing a soft green and tan skirt and jacket over a white turtleneck, she was sure that he didn't stand a chance. His heart had found a match and it really was that obvious.

"We have a 6:30 reservation at Ernie's Steak House, so we won't be late," he murmured toward Sue. With a lingering look toward Chris, he said even softer, "You look stunning."

As Sue closed the door she was nearly laughing out loud. He didn't stand a chance.

On the way to Ernie's, he was sharing information about his family. "Dad has a heating and cooling company in Richardson, Texas and my little sister is his bookkeeper. Mom has always been a homemaker and she is still busy as a volunteer at church and the GOP. Patrick, my big brother is on the faculty at TCU so the folks are all pretty close. I've been in the Corps for eight years and it feels like a career." When he looked at her she was aware that he was waiting for her information.

She gave the bare overview of disintegration and separation. "When I was eighteen I came to Chico to be a live-in nanny and student for the Meyers." Randall glanced at her in surprise. "Yeah, it got real complicated when Clara was killed," Chris said in a small voice.

They were in the restaurant parking lot so he said, "Let's go inside to finish that account. It must have been agony for you all. How old was Julie?"

Chris didn't move toward the door. Instead, she placed her hand on Randall's shoulder and said quietly, "Thank you for taking the high ground. Most folks who hear that much of the story, leap to erroneous conclusions."

When they were seated they both ordered iced tea and she continued, "Bruce Meyers was a brave and honorable man. Our relationship was basically business; I was to be Julie's companion until she went to college. When he proposed marriage I was shocked but soon understood it was a mantle of protection for his daughter. If something terrible happened to him she would be powerless to defend herself or his estate. There was no intimacy in our marriage and for sure nothing to be ashamed about. You met the Wilsons. Perry was Bruce's copilot. He was asked to stand down from that last flight so the helicopter could go faster and use less fuel as the bomb was being moved out to sea. I have always believed that was a selfless act on Bruce's part because he knew the terrible risk he was taking. They are sharing the big house with Julie and me to assist and comfort us. I've never known truer friends."

She took a big breath and asked, "So, how has your day been, Charlie?"

"I can tell you," his smiling face looked at her, "that my day has become reasonably better just hearing some of the challenges you have overcome and maintained a positive attitude in the process. There are a couple little safeguards I must clear up, however." He waited for her to take a sip of tea. "I use the name Charles Randall when I'm not sure of the situation. My given name is Randall Howe and my partner is Denny McFarland. His dad played baseball for the Washington Senators." He sighed and said, "After our first meeting I promised myself that there would always be only the truth between us. I think you are an outstanding person and I hope you will allow me to get to know you better."

"Thank you, sir," she said with a radiant smile. "When I speak with our Japanese friend I always call him Mr. Edward because his last name is hard to remember and harder to pronounce. I think I would rather call you Mr. Randall than Randy. That makes me think of a condition rather than an individual." There was even a soft laugh after her admission.

"O.K." he moved a bit closer as though he wanted no one to eavesdrop. "By any wild chance in the world, is your brother's name Michael Winter?"

"How could you know that? Yes it is, but I..." She wasn't sure what to say.

Randall put his hand on her arm reassuringly. "Please don't be alarmed. It was your 'Stars and little fishes' at our previous conversation that caught my attention. I've never heard another soul say that except my squad leader for the past four years. It shocked me when you said it and you even used the same voice inflections. I knew at that moment that my heart was in big trouble. He is like a big brother to me; I think the world of him and trust him with my life. So now you know some of the reasons why I am so attracted to you too." He removed his hand from her arm but not his gaze. Neither of them spoke for several seconds.

Chris broke the long pause by saying softly, "Our dad used that phrase when he wanted to swear without using profanity. It reminds me of a happy time in my childhood." Her smile grew a bit flirty and she whispered, "I'm glad you have more than one reason to be attracted. I was charmed when you didn't get all defensive when I was snarky at our introduction. So I'm attracted too."

Chris ordered chicken strips with fries so she could nibble and chat. Randall ordered a medium rare steak with a mashed potatoe so he could eat and listen. She told him that he was racking up points as the perfect date.

He kept that winning streak going by asking if she had chosen her Master's Thesis. That impressed her. "So far it's just a general outline, but I think there is something very noteworthy in it," When he raised his eyebrows suggesting that he was indeed listening, she went on. "I've been thinking about an alternative to our prison system. It seems to me we are merely warehousing people in a less than ideal situation. They come out after serving their time in worse condition than they went in and are unprepared to be productive citizens. There must be a better way."

Randall had become so captured by her thought, he wasn't even eating. "That's a very large subject to tackle."

"I know," Chris said happily. "That's what makes it so captivating. My plan has four parts that will cover at least two years. The female candidates would be carefully screened so they could live in a low security building."

"Hey," he interrupted. "Why female? The guys need help too."

"Yes, they do," she answered with a big smile. "But their crimes are usually more serious. They are more aggressive and the prospects of housing them in low security is problematic. For my test run I chose females. Ideally there would be at least twenty. The first two weeks would be getting them clean and sober from drugs or alcohol. They would address their addiction. The second phase could be added simultaneously with another two week extension. It would run maybe two months, repairing their bodies with diet and exercise. They would learn the benefits of lots of water, rest and good nutrition. The third phase would offer technical training; you know, culinary, office, computer, anything that would get them employable. They could even get a GED if they needed one. I'm thinking that could last two years. The fourth phase would be learning to fill out an application and interview for employment. Graduation, or parole would be more accurate, would be when they are employed. They would need to meet any parole conditions, of course."

She was about to continue but Randall asked, "I don't hear anything like a penalty for their law-breaking. Is there some punishment in your plan?"

"Good question," she said brightly. "I believe in restitution for the victim, if that is appropriate. That can happen only if they are given skills and opportunity to earn. Think of a child who breaks a glass; there are some parents who might punish the careless child. Good ones however, teach the child how to be more responsible. There is a world of difference between retribution and rehabilitation."

Randall nodded in both understanding and agreement.

Chris continued, "The benefits from this plan are obvious. A person is assisted in becoming a useful part of society instead of a likely reoffender. But more practically, once we have a facility, the annual savings would be tenfold. Instead of the current institutional nine hundred forty thousand dollars a year to house twenty, this program will run efficiently at ninety thousand.

"I've been thinking it should be called 'Second Chance'" she said, "because we all need one. It would need some teeth to keep folks honest of course. A doctor would do a weekly drug test for each student with zero tolerance for violation. Fights or weapons would have the same consideration, as would sneaking in a playmate. Violators would be moved immediately back to general population with no consideration for early release. Someone else would get a second chance in their place." Chris realized how much she had been rattling along so she shyly said, "I've been thinking about it a lot. I'm not sure you were prepared for the whole bucket."

"I'm thinking what a great concept that is. Once again I am aware of your kind spirit. Most of us would like to flush convicts, if we think of them at all. They are more like a troublesome nuisance rather than a person who never learned the respect of boundaries. You have imagined a wholesome and beneficial overhaul. I think you are right in saying men would be more problematic. But for the ones who might see the benefit, a second chance would be life-changing. For many of us the military is a great place to learn discipline and respect for others. I hope you can find a way to make your plan work."

Chris was encouraged by his appraisal. Thoughtfully she said, "I suppose the first challenge will be to find an old hotel or apartment house that could be given an overhaul to accommodate the idea." She took another bite of chicken and advised him that the food was getting cold with all this talk. Small talk was the applied activity through the rest of the main course. As the desserts were being served, she asked if he had any travel plans.

Randall knew he was about to cross a Corps line, but he was building a sense of trust with her and so he said in a more confidential voice, "Michael has ordered a very brief and unofficial trip across into Mexico. We have some unfinished business that has become a high priority to him. Lt. Colonel Sherman, our Commander, has given us a green light but requested no specifics. Maybe at another dinner in the future I will be able to tell you more."

"That sounds like the sort of pressure release Bruce loved after an ATF mission, she replied in the same confidential manner. "Sometime he would have a couple beers and get talkative, but he was always careful not to disclose details. I really miss both of those wonderful people." Her face was suddenly lost in memories.

Randall leaned over and whispered, "You provide the beer and I'll tell you all about it. This one is going to be big." Delightful small-talk filled the rest of their time. If you would have asked them about a topic, they would have answered, "I can't really tell you. It was just delightful."

As he walked Chris back up to her front door, he said with a bit of a Texas drawl, "Mama always told me to never let a girl kiss me on our first date. But she did say that the girl could give me a hug, if she really wanted too." With a bit of a giggle, Chris wrapped her arms around him and they both were thrilled by the warmth and firmness of the embrace.

She said, "Give me a day's warning when you will be available for another dinner in Chico and I will be delighted to fix my favorite."

"Oooo, that sounds mysterious," he answered immediately. "What is it?"

"There is a brand new meat package," she said with a hushed voice, " called SPAM. I can do wonders with it." Their laughter was as enjoyable as a kiss. Not really, but for this evening they both agreed it was a perfect conclusion.

The MST (Mobile Strike Team) left Coronado at 1500 aboard a UH 60 long range Black Hawk helicopter. Ninety percent of the flight plan was over U.S. soil. South of Carrizo Springs, Texas, however, they flew due south toward Guadalupe, Mexico to finish a job. Intelligence had confirmed that the drug lord known as Antonio Ruise, along with a dozen or more of his cohorts were gathered there. Using a low mountain range to reduce the sound of their approach on whisper mode, the team was able then to make the final mile on foot in the gathering twilight.

"There is enough breeze to aim a controlled fire," Michael said softly. "Lee and Robert, work your way around to the front and set the brush fire upwind of the place. Make sure you are wide enough to hit them squarely. The rest of us will breach the back door just like we did last time. Once again we are not here to capture. Don't let anyone sneak passed you." He looked from face to face receiving an understanding nod, Fifteen minutes later with only a few stars in the darkening sky, a heavy plume of smoke was noticed by the gate guards. They sounded the alarm and died in the same breath. A growing number of panicked men rushed out to battle the growing blaze unaware that the true threat was closing in on them from the cover of distraction. It was a full assault with silenced weapons. This time Michael wanted to make sure that the snake and his cronies were dead. The battle was over in less than five minutes. Bodies were moved inside the compound as the flames drew closer.

A quick survey of the building discovered the drug storage and the phenomenal hoard of cash. Once again Michael was pouring gas on the drugs as he said, "Gather whatever you choose to carry out. Set the timer on your grenades for ten minutes and let's beat feet." Each man was stuffing his field pack with one hundred dollar bills, Michael and Randall also crammed their duffle bags full as they heard the distant whine of a siren.

Before the fire truck arrived, eight grenades, several pounds of C4 along with the propane tank near the back wall, turned the cocaine headquarters into a crater. There is no way to know how many men lost their life nor how much cash was incinerated. There was also no tally of the amount the team was able to carry back to "cover their expenses." Ethics is a challenging subject. Is it better to destroy clandestine money rather than to use it for a more fulfilling retirement? The team slept on their way home, each with a comfortable pillow of cash.

Before the Easter break, Mrs. Russell called again. "Chris you are my go-to-girl. We need a blog for the June Log. Do you think there is room in your busy schedule for another terrific article?"

"Am I correct in thinking the due date is the second week in May?" she asked, implying acceptance.

"You are the best!" the grateful registrar giggled. "I look forward to your thoughts."

"Be your own BFF. Submitted by Chris Meyers.

"The author of the Book of Ecclesiastes took a rather dim view of the whole human enterprise. I sometimes wonder how that book was ever canonized. Curiously however, he succeeded in pressing 'the wine of good hope' from 'the grapes of wrath.' Even though he considered the human effort a vain striving after the wind, he was spiritually and psychologically correct when he wrote, 'Whatsoever your hand finds to do, do it with all your might.' Plainly the seer knew, perhaps from personal experience, that work half-done is a spiritual liability, leaving shame and regret as the sad finality.

"We need to be aware that the unturned stone may hide buried treasure. The experiment not tried may hold some creative secret for the chemist. The extra effort not given by the athlete may very well mean the difference between a win or a loss. 'Leave no stone unturned ' is another way of saying 'Whatsoever your hand finds to do, do it with all your might.'

"We all know that one of the most depressing of life's experiences is regret. In fact, someone has said, 'Hell is the specter of our wasted opportunities. Hell is the memory of the 'little more ' we did not give or the stone we did not turn.' We failed here or there not because failure was written in our stars, but rather because we did not demand enough of ourselves. Said another way, successful people do what the failures don't like to do. Succeeding in life is really nothing more than doing everything we have to do in the best way we can and finishing the job.

"It's not too late in this spring quarter; it's never too late to change! Ask yourself : am I demanding enough of myself? What can I do to increase my personal productivity? Do I have a stone unturned?"

Be your own BFF!

"Moshi moshi, Chris san. It is your admiring dinner partner, Randall san."

"Good afternoon. "I'm impressed with your Japanese. I take it that you had a successful mission." She didn't want to pry for information.

"It was a super successful trip. Now I wonder if you have an evening available for us to dine together again."

"It just so happens, sir, that both Friday and Saturday are free from obligations. I've planned hamburgers for Friday and Sue has had a bumper week so I thought steaks would be appropriate for Saturday. Julie would prefer another quarter pounder. Would you care to join us? You can have your choice." Her tone was warm and playful.

"I would love to join you," he said happily. "May I bring the steaks and help with the barbecue?" He wanted to be sure she understood his willingness to contribute. "I've also found a couple old apartment houses that you might be interested in. I'll bring the details. What time shall I be there?"

"Well, as long as you are cooking," she said, "anytime after 4:00 o'clock. Wait, I mean any time after 1600. I'll fix us an appetizer."

"There you go. I'm feeling more at home every time we get together. I'll see you then."

With a girlish giggle Chris said, "Roger that. Chris Out." They were both chuckling as they hung up.

The marvelous dinner was finished, right down to the frozen chocolate éclairs. Sue had explained how the Japanese golfers worked and Perry had filled him in on the ATF relationship to National Security. Finally Julie asked Sue if she would be interested in hearing a Berenstain Bear book. There were still several she had not read. Sue excused them and Perry took advantage of the break to go along with them. Conveniently Chris and Randall were left at the table with many unfinished conversations.

"How is your Ma..." he began to ask a question as she did as well, "How do you..." They both laughed at their eagerness to continue the table talk. She motioned for him to go ahead.

"I was going to ask about your thesis. Are you still going after a prison alternative?" His smile was relaxed and Chris was delighted to tell him about her accomplishments.

"I was able to get a bit of a jump start by taking two of my required subjects in the spring quarter. I'm sure that by this time next year the Master's will be accomplished. I even had two calls from state HR folks who are looking for department directors in DSHS.

With a surprised look, he asked, "Does that mean you are not going to pursue your correction thesis?"

She shrugged and said, "The thesis is conceptual. It does not depend on a working model to be accepted." She leaned a bit closer to him and said, "If I could create a working model, I would probably want to sell it to the state rather that go into the business of correction reform."

Randall reached over to the table for his notebook. "I found two hotels in the metro LA area that you might want to look at. The one in Compton has a capacity of forty rooms. There is some fire damage and lots of trash from squatters, so it's pretty cheap, it seems to me." He spread a sales picture and description. As Chris came around to his side of the table and leaned against him so she could get a good look, he smiled contentedly. That contact hadn't been in his plan, but oh my, it was nice.

"This second one," he unfolded another sheet, "is in Culver City. Some time ago it was a luxury hotel. The neighborhood changed and the ownership did too. The formal dining room became a bar and dance floor. The place was raided several times for operating as a brothel. It was in the hands of the court for several years and is now a target for a complete tear-down but I believe it could receive a second chance."

Chris said, "It looks to be five or six floors. That's probably way too large for my test effort. Besides, where would I get all the money it would take to restore such a place?"

"Good point," Randall said with a secret smile. "But if you don't mind, I'll keep looking. We might just find a gem." She had no way of knowing that he was thinking about the bags of money he had recently liberated.

Chris moved back to the other side of the table so she could look directly at him. "Hey," she asked, "how is it that you are working so often in Sacramento but billeted in San Diego? Do you have quarters in both cities? Isn't it a long day's drive between the two?"

He nodded and said, "It would be a long 500 mile day for sure. NSA California has its main office near the state buildings in downtown Sacramento. There are three or four shuttle flights each day between Coronado and the Executive Field up here. That's not part of the International Field, south east of the city. I can hop a flight whenever I need to come up here for reports or assignments. It is only about a 60 minute trip each way."

She was ready to ask another question, but he wanted to talk about her week instead, so he asked Chris, "Can you recall something this week that made you laugh?"

Immediately she said, "Julie and I laugh all the time. She has a wonderful curiosity and sense of humor." Then she thought of something else. "My Admin professor is Dr. Shannon Pierce, and students often say, behind her back of course, that she is fierce Pierce. Yesterday she had written on the overhead, 'give me two reason why you shouldn't teach a pig to sing.' We didn't know if she was joking or looking for an application of some training principles. I decided to answer '1. Pigs do not have mouth and lip structures to sing; and 2. Pigs must first be taught to speak in English.' She had a big smile, which we had rarely seen, when she informed us that we had just finished the chapter on responsible time use.

"This exercise was a summation of all that we had read. The correct answers were, 1. It only wastes your time; and 2. It only annoys the pig.' She concluded her lecture by saying that she hoped we had not been annoyed by it. Those of us who realized she had just made a pig reference, cracked up. It was super humorous." She smiled and turned the question back to him, asking, "Has anything made you laugh this week? So much of your tasks are dangerous and nasty."

"Well…" He wasn't quite sure how to express it, "whenever

I see my squad leader I feel like smiling or laughing because I have intentionally not told him that the reason for my frequent Sacramento trips is my growing interest in his sister. I'm afraid he might crack me on the side of my head."

"Are you really that sure he is my brother?" she asked again.

"No doubt about it," Randall replied confidently. "Michael G. Winter was born 5/3/73 in Everett, Washington. He's our man."

"How much longer do you think you can keep that secret?" Her smile suggested that she found it humorous also.

"Well..." He still wasn't sure how to express it. "I hope we might reach a day when we will want him to know.... and bless us." The smile grew even larger.

A couple hours later, after the dishes, a Berenstain Bear story, some conversation about the golfers, and school and a hint of the future, Randall was preparing to leave when he mentioned that Sherman has made another clandestine mission. "We were told to be ready to depart tomorrow evening. A drug source in Puerto Rico with supplies from Jamaica requires our attention. I'll be gone a couple days at least. Our Lt. Colonel will be taking an advancement and he wants to go out with a bang." He shook Perry's hand and hugged Sue. "Thank you for another gracious supper. It was outstanding." As he gave Chris an embrace he added, "This is better home-cooking than I've ever had. Thank you for including me." The other three smiled warmly knowing that he wanted to say so much more.

It was the end of the spring quarter and Chris knew she needed a break. With Sue's assurance that everything was in order with the golfers, Chris and Julie were eager to spend a long weekend with Gram Holly and Grampa Jeff.

Chris loved the flight-path into Seattle. The plane was over water, then land and just as quickly more water. She saw the Space Needle and more water; then they were suddenly at the airport. She was puzzled though about the twilight. The sun had been setting as they left Chico and here there was still enough daylight to see distant mountains. The happy grandparents chased that curiosity away for a moment with their delighted greeting.

"No, just these carry-on," Chris replied. "With this nice summer weather, we thought we could get along with shorts and light tops." Julie had not released her embrace of Gram Holly. Both of them were near tears of delight. "If we need to be more dressed up, we can go to a thrift shop."

Holly said in an excited voice, "Saturday afternoon we are invited to a GOP zip code meeting. Director Suzanne Murphy has invited the registered republicans of Shoreline to an informational get-together. Jeff wants me to go for once because a door prize of a one year free subscription to Sirius Radio is offered to those who attend. He said he would take Julie to either the zoo or the aquarium, whichever she would like. I just think it would be a great opportunity to meet some new folks and learn about current issues. It would only take a couple hours."

Chris wanted to ease any hesitance Holly might be feeling, so smiling, she said, "I would really like to become more informed about local politics. I'm thinking that in another year, Julie and I are going to relocate closer to you."

"Really?" a delighted Grandmother exclaimed. "That is terrific news! The housing market is pretty tight right now, but there are always places to look at." She hooked her arm inside Chris's. "I can't tell you how much we miss Clara, and how brave we think you have been caring for Julie. You make our hearts happy again."

"Well maybe you can tell me," the happy visitor asked, "why do you still have daylight and its dark in Chico?"

Holly pursed her lips and said lightly, "We're special. After enduring a nine month winter, we have to get extra sunshine to make up for what we missed." Chris nudged her with a happy elbow. "No, seriously, if you think about the basic geography," Holly said wisely. "Seattle is about two thirds of the way from the equator towards the North Pole, where summer days never get completely dark. We get about sixteen hours of daylight each day this month; just eight hours of dark. In December it is just opposite. The sun comes up about eight o'clock and goes down by four in the afternoon. That makes for great sleeping in and late breakfasts."

Chris and Julie shared a happy glance. It was so good to be with family again.

Friday was a leisurely day with only a few errands and a Red Robin hamburger supper. Now as Chris scanned the room of about a hundred folks, she was grateful for the Value Village thrift store. She had found an attractive blue dress and shoes with an accent red and white silk scarf. She looked every bit the patriot. As she listened to the attractive lady who had identified herself as the Chairman of the state Republican Party, Chris felt impressed and glad that she so blended with the crowd.

Imagine her shock as she heard that lady express gratitude to the host of the activities, Ward Winter! "No way!" she thought to herself. "What would the odds be?" But when he stood to welcome the gathering, she could recognize her little brother right down to the scar on his chin. He had been so roughed up and yet stayed moxie. She scarcely listened to the presentations, her eyes fastened on that handsome young man. She could see the likeness of her dad! Tears began to form in her eyes as she thought, "I have family here! He is my brother!"

As the gathering was disbursing, Holly was having some difficulty following the claim that Chris was related to their host. She patiently waited for the crowd to clear.

"Mr. Winter, you cannot imagine how delighted I am to

greet you. It has been about twenty five years since we were last together. One of mom's many boyfriends was shaking you like a rag toy. That's a rough memory to hold all these years. I do believe you have a sister named Chrissy. That's me, now all grown up." She held out her hand. He hesitated then shook her hand politely, then tugged her into an embrace.

"I never expected to see you again," he said softly. "It was such a crazy time." He reluctantly released her and they began to rebuild their understanding of two and a half decades. All the while Holly stood and listened in wonder.

Finally Ward's hospitality thought to invite the ladies upstairs to meet Becky and Sophie.

"Who is Sophie?" Chris asked in delight. "Is there even more surprise in this afternoon?"

"Sophie is Becky's eight year old daughter, who I was fortunate enough to adopt with our wedding."

With a sweet smile, Chris said, "What a coincidence; I have an adopted daughter who will turn seven in September."

Ward frowned slightly as he asked, "How in the world could that happen?"

"Well," Chris began, "I was employed to be a nanny. A horrible series of events made me her adopted mom. It has been a blessing for us in spite of two tragedies."

Holly added quietly, "Clara, Julie's mom, was my daughter. Chris's integrity and commitment has been inspiring. As they say, 'It's a long story.'"

Once again Ward was mindful of his hospitality. "Is there a Grandpa Windsor and may I invite them to join us here for some pizza?"

"There is," Holly said happily. "I'll call his cell phone because they are probably still at the aquarium. It's nice of you to offer the invitation." The prospects of continued reunion were welcome but perhaps not as much as two young ladies anticipated the prospect of meeting a new cousin.

The Bell Black Hawk took off from Coronado with a compliment of nine agents, a full house. Six hours later they landed in Pensacola to refuel. As soon as they were refreshed they took off again, this time due south over the Gulf of Mexico. When they were clear of the west end of Cuba they turned east once again and about 0230 they landed in a school yard in Port Antonio, Jamaica. Their target was a nondescript house about a half mile away near the outskirts. The team that entered the front door found a sleeping guard, who never had an opportunity to sound an alarm. The team that breached the back door interrupted a poker game. Seven or eight silenced pistol shots were nearly instantaneous. Again there was no alarm. The house was scoured finding little resistance; six more men were quietly killed in their bed. The team's target was the laboratory in the basement that processed the white powder. There were sacks of material and containers of heroine. In a separate room there were boxes of cash, lots of boxes.

"You know the drill, gentlemen," Michael said quietly. "Set C4 at all corners; incendiary grenades set for 15 minutes on my mark. We don't have gas for this one so place a brick of C4 under the smack. We want it to burn. Take what you choose to carry." He turned and began filling his field pack. About four minutes later he asked, "All set?" He was looking for raised fists in acknowledgement. "On my mark," there was a tiny hesitation. "Mark!" With timers all set they made their way out of the house and back toward the Black Hawk double time. Michael noticed that Randall had a full pack and he was carrying a full box as well.

The Black Hawk was just clearing the school yard when a bright finger of fire pierced the night and the ominous roll of thunder rumbled the town awake. There were a few citizens who thought they saw the aircraft depart but more thought that a spaceship of some sort had caused the destruction. Most just knew that the "factory" was destroyed and there would be hell to pay.

"Good job, y'all," Michael's strong voice carried above the engine's roar. "We have four hours before the second half of the job. Get something to eat, water up and get a nap if you can. The next one is going to be in daylight so they will be ready for us. Tank, you and Glen will man the 50.s. We need you to shoot the shit out of the doors and windows for about a minute. Then we'll roll in. I want all the rest of the C4 we have and all the grenades set with a ten minute timer. This is a quick hit and go. This may be our last op together if Sherman is leaving, so let's show him we are the best at what we do." The roar of the engines and the resolve of the strong men made a symphony of battle as the Black Hawk hurried toward the dawning of another day.

Port Patillas is a picturesque setting on the southeast corner of Puerto Rico. Recon informed Michael that their target was situated on a hillside that gave the Black Hawk enough cover to set down within a couple hundred yards of the house. "We will probably have company as soon as we set down," Michael warned. "So use both doors to deploy. Fifties first and immediately light them up. We don't have a head count but this is a principle source of coke so there will be a crowd. I do not want to take any C4 or grenades back to Coronado. We brought it here to do a job so use it all; ETA is fourteen minutes so get ready to rumble!"

Tense moments later the pilot shouted, "ETA is nine minutes!"

These were warriors who were familiar with the rush of adrenalin and rapid heartbeat. Each had his own technique for managing the moment of engagement.

"Target in sight," the pilot called.

In a cloud of dust, the helicopter touched down and the men poured out. Within a few seconds sporadic defensive fire came from the house and was answered by the devastating roar of the 50.s. The right side of the team moved rapidly up the hill to cover any attempt to flee out the back. Two crouching forms made a break for it and fell immediately. After a minute of punishment the assault rifles were still and the team moved to breach all doors. The battle was brief and very one-sided. The dead were placed in the center of the house as room by room was cleared. As before the basement was a treasure trove of bags of drug material and cash. As the team gathered, happy for no casualties, they found the money contained in large nylon sports bags, an entire wall covered by the pile.

"You know what to do," Michael barked. "Get those bricks …." He didn't finish the C4 order. A very large man had hidden behind a false wall and now rushed out. He was swinging a machete at the closest neck near him, which happened to be Randall's!

"Down!" was all Michael could shout as his 45. jerked up and two rounds were fired lethally. The muzzle flash was right beside Randall's face. He flinched from the heat and explosive sound, which may have saved his life. Both rounds hit the head of the attacking man, spinning him somewhat off his target. But his momentum continued and he crashed against Randall. They all saw the razor-sharp blade chop into the back of his leg just above his calf and his knee suddenly folded unnaturally. A scream of pain was cut short as the bulk of disaster fell on him buckling the table covered with heroine. Randall's head thumped on the concrete floor in a cloud of white dust, followed by a heartbeat of silence.

Michael rolled the dead body off his unconscious friend. He immediately saw arterial bleeding and shouted, "Get those timers set for ten on my count. Now! Take what you can carry and burn everything in this room!" He removed Randall's pant leg and with his belt he fashioned a tourniquet then lifted him to his shoulder and moved toward the Black Hawk. Someone shouted, "Make sure to take a bag for the boss or Randall and one for the pilot!" Most of the team that ran to their copter had a sport bag in each hand.

The propellers were already at full speed as the last man scrambled aboard. They were airborne less than a minute when the house erupted in a cloud of fire and splinters.

Michael shouted to the pilot, "The nearest American hospital is in Charlotte Amalie on St. Thomas. We should be there in fifteen minutes, Head east by southeast until you can establish your course." The copilot was already working on their GPS.

"Charlotte Amalie Tower, this is Military Black Hawk Coronado 1, over." The pilot repeated the call twice before he had an answer. "This is Amalie Tower; over"

"Amalie Tower this is Coronado 1 declaring a medical emergency. Request you divert all commercial traffic away in six minutes. Contact Charlotte Amalie Hospital we are arriving at the helipad with an arterial injury. Over."

There was a pause of about thirty seconds before the answer. "Coronado 1, traffic is being diverted and the hospital is standing by. Over."

"Amalie Tower, we have you in sight. Thanks for the assistance. Coronado 1, out."

Their pilot demonstrated outstanding skill as he wheeled around and touched down gently, placing Randall's door next to the waiting gurney. The hospital team took over very aware of the drug covered unconscious victim and weapons still evident. A doctor inspecting the wound asked, "Whose idea was the duct tape?"

"That would be mine, sir. It seemed like a way to reduce leakage. Warrant Officer Michael Winter, sir. I'm in charge of this mission, which is still an active NSA Drug Interdiction. You were the nearest American Hospital I could think of." He was liberally splattered by blood from his shoulder to his knees. "Gunnery Sergeant Randall Howe is our wounded, sir. If you will give me a contact person we will take care of the paperwork later. We still have a mission to complete."

The doctor looked at the weapons still in plain sight

and the blood splatters on every one of the men. This was obviously not a time to dally with details. He shook Michael's hand saying, "I admire your call to duty, sir. Your care for a fallen brother is the stuff legends are made of. Semper fi, sir."

"Thank you, sir. I'll be back here in a couple days to take him home. Don't let him trick you into giving him a bunch of painkillers. He's tougher than a boot heel."

The doctor stammered, "But he won't be ready to go home for quite some time."

"If you will make sure he doesn't bleed to death and do what you can with that machete bite, we'll get him to a military hospital to fix his wheel." He saluted the doctor, or perhaps the still form on its way into the hospital; then he turned and reentered the Black Hawk.

The pilot said, "Amalie Tower this is Coronado 1 ready for departure, over."

"Coronado 1 this is Amalie Tower, you are clear to depart; we currently have no inbound traffic, over.

"Amalie Tower this is Coronado 1, roger that. Thanks for your hospitality, Coronado 1, out." The Black Hawk demonstrated its agility again as it gracefully rose and briskly headed north by northwest toward the eastern end of Cuba. From there it would be a couple hours to Pensacola, a fresh tank of fuel for all involved and then home.

When Lt. Colonel Sherman called the next day to determine Sgt. Howe's condition, he was told that a six hour procedure last night had successfully repaired the damage to Randall. "We understood the urgency of his condition and called the VA Navy Hospital in Baltimore for assistance. Dr. Cyrus Peterson their chief of surgery and his team were flown down and conducted the repair. As they say, 'If you can't get the patient to the doctor, get the doctor to the patient.' I'll tell you that officer in charge of the squad was a quick thinker to bring sergeant Howe here. In another few minutes he would have bled out. It was touch and go for a bit as it was. You can tell his team that he is resting after the ordeal and will be ready to move in a couple weeks, wearing a full leg cast."

Chaplain White called Chris in the afternoon. "Don't be alarmed," he said. "I'm just relaying a message from a Staff Sergeant Denny McFarland. He wants you to know that one of his squad members, a Gunnery Sergeant Randall Howe, was injured on their recent mission. His knee was banged up and they had to leave him in St. Thomas at Charlotte Amalie Hospital, among a lot of pretty ladies and waving palm trees, or maybe it was waving ladies and pretty palm trees. I think he made up the last part, but he was pretty sure that Sgt. Howe would like you to know and not worry if he misses a Friday night supper." The chaplain paused and then said playfully, "that sounds like your social life has improved."

Chris laughed sweetly, "Anything added to zero is an improvement. So yes, we have had a couple dinners out and he has been a welcomed guest at the house two or three times. We have enjoyed some long phone conversations so I'll see if I can get in touch with him and find out about those pretty ladies. Thanks for passing the message along." She smiled thinking that was the closest she could come to speaking with her other brother without doing it face to face. She was pretty sure that would happen one day soon.

Her first two phone calls were frustrating. A nurse simply told her that the patient was not receiving calls. She should try again tomorrow. On day three her call was answered by a very drowsy, "Hello…. This is Gunnery Sergeant Howe."

"There's that big guy I've been anxious to talk to," she said playfully. "Hi, it's your dining partner Chris."

Another long pause before he said, "Hello back at'cha." She could hear him draw in a deep breath. "The nurse told me my honey called twice." His speech was still slow but it was evident he was trying to perk up. "And here you are, Honey. I'm happy to hear your voice. It has been quite an"…. another labored breath … "interesting three days."

"Listen big guy, I want you to save your strength to get well. Just know that I am praying for your recovery, and eager to see your cute face. I'll call back in a few days to applaud your progress. This is Chris at Chico 1, out."

As he handed the phone back to the nurse, she wasn't sure whether he was smiling or wincing in pain. His contented hum convinced her it was a smile after all. The recovery plan for Randall was three more weeks in Charlotte Amalie then a six week recovery furlough in Dallas. It would be late August before he was back on limited active desk duty and by then his MST unit would be working out of the Pentagon in Washington D.C. without Warrant Officer Michael Winter, who would be the only remaining NCO in Coronado. Lt. Colonel Dwight Blakely would replace Sherman, with a completely different understanding of his purpose. There would be no clandestine operations on foreign soil and most definitely no domestic operation without warrants and due process. LT. Col. Blakely assigned Winter to port surveillance, which meant wandering around acres of cargo containers at night in the hopes of stumbling on criminal activity. One thing you can say about the Corps: when they screw up, it is big time for sure! Michael was convinced it was time for him to seek another career path. He had heard the Secret Service needed good men.

A warm June turned into a hot July in Chico. The heat would have been much worse were it not for the new air conditioner that was installed and the fact that Perry made sure the family was at the base pool each afternoon. In many ways it was a tranquil time. Perhaps there were moments of exception to that when Chris was struggling with a summer intensive graduate class on Tax Code. She was amazed that there were so many ways to avoid or defer tax payments. In fact, Perry and Sue had her revamp their savings program now that amazing funds were pouring in from the golfers. She recalled her advice to Bruce about investing in thirty year Treasuries. "Those even fly under the bank auditor's radar if you are using golfer funds to pay for them." That information would become very important in the future.

For Randall a fuzzy June ended with an ambulance ride to the Charlotte Amalie airport where a sleek Bombardier Learjet awaited his arrival. He was hesitant to board the plane thinking it might be an angry drug Lord seeking revenge, until he saw that the crew was U.S. military. He didn't ask whose aircraft it might be because he was pretty sure it wasn't military issue. The extra wide seat allowed him and his cumbersome cast to buckle up in comfort for the three hour flight to Dallas, where another ambulance awaited his arrival. As he deplaned, Randall shook the hands of the three man crew as they thanked him for his service and sacrifice.

As soon as he was home, greeted by an over-attentive mom, he called Chris. "I just wanted you to know that I am home for the next six weeks. Maybe you can thank the chaplain for me. Chaplain White called me a few times and even prayed with me before a couple of the surgeries. He sent me a book to read"

"Are you comfortable; is there anything you need?" Chris asked happily. "It is so good to hear you have progressed this much. How was the plane ride from St. Thomas?" she had so many questions. "It is just so good to hear your strong voice."

"I know," he said happily, "It's as sweet as candy to hear your voice too. I could gain back some of the weight I've lost last month."

"I could fix you my famous SPAM dinner that usually adds muscle." Her voice was nearly laughing, which was all the medicine he needed.

"Listen, I've been thinking it will be easy for me to over-stay my welcome on your phone, so how about letting me call you? That way the monumental bill will come to me instead of you."

"I don't mind paying my share," she countered. "It does my heart good to hear from you." She was a bit confused by the suggestion. She hoped it wasn't because he was losing interest in their budding relationship.

"Good, I'm glad we agree that I will call you, but not more than twice a day. Here's mom's number." He repeated it to make sure she had it. "One other detail for today. Would it be a great inconvenience to store a half dozen bulky items at your place? They are too cumbersome to move to D.C. right now. Sherman is moving the MST to the pentagon and I just don't know what to do about that. Maybe we can chat about that soon. Denny could drop them off at your place if you agree. You know they are about the size of a couple field packs, my duffle, a box and a couple more sport bags. Is there some out of the way spot for those?"

She smiled as she said, "Of course we can store your stuff here. There is an extra closet in the basement that would be safe and secure as well as out of the way." Her joy was in the fact that not only was he not losing interest, this felt like the first part of moving in. "When do you imagine he can bring those things?"

"He's planning to be there just before supper tomorrow. Maybe he could enjoy your SPAM supper." His voice got sort of breathy.

She could tell he was finding a lot of humor in this. "Oh darn it," she murmured. "Our menu is for meatloaf with twice-baked potatoes. But he will be welcome to rough it with us for sure."

"Now you're just teasing me," Randall growled. "If I didn't have this cast, I'd make it there myself."

Softly in a flirty voice, Chris answered, "Now look who is teasing. It will be so wonderful when I get to see you again."

"I'll call you about 1800 just to make sure everything went

as planned, and maybe to get a whiff of meatloaf. I just love it and I'm pretty darned happy when I'm with you too."

"Roger that, this is Chico 1, out." They were both smiling broadly.

The next afternoon as the happy group was heading toward the base swimming pool the chaplain waved and redirected his path to join them. "Hi Chris," he said in greeting. "I haven't heard a current update, but I think Randall is coming along just fine and will soon be released to recuperate at home."

Her happy reply was evidence that the relationship was genuine, "He's already home in Dallas. I chatted with him yesterday."

"That is such good news." The chaplain's evident joy may have been due to Chris's obvious pleasure as much as concern for a wounded warrior. "I sent him a book to read during his furlough; it's entitled 'Christians Under Construction,' written by a pastor named Mark Duncan. If you would like to read along with him I have a copy for you as well."

She thanked him for the gracious thoughtfulness. "I can imagine that will be welcomed information for both of us." She didn't want to admit that her spiritual life had been painfully neglected. This would be a marvelous opportunity to improve that oversight.

When the phone rang about 4 o'clock, she thought it must be Randall who forgot about the two time-zone difference. Instead Mrs. Russell's familiar voice was soliciting another blog for the Log. "I'm pretty sure this is about as far as I can stretch our friendship. Can you have something for our August pre-session edition, something about enthusiasm?"

"This is a timely call," Chris replied happily. "I've been thinking about this whole education experience and how grateful I am about it. I can have a copy on your desk by

Friday. How about that?" Chris was feeling unusually playful for some reason.

"Chris, you are an angel for sure. I wish you were on staff here. Is that something you might be interested in?" The registrar was not accustomed to give that much praise or employment suggestions.

Brightly Chris answered, "I have no idea what I will be doing this time next year, but I'm pretty sure it will be in cooler Seattle. I'll get right on the blog."

Be your own BFF submitted by Chris Meyers

'What are you working towards? Is it worthy of your powers? Does it call forth the best that's in you every day? Is it a great and constant vision before your eyes? What motivates you?

If I asked you to go out and run a mile, would you do it? Would you run a mile right now for a dollar? I didn't think so. But what if I offered you a thousand dollars? What if I convinced you that the life of someone you love depended on it? Would you run then? You would run a mile with all your might, wouldn't you? It all depends on one word *motivation!*

If someone offered you a job as his representative in France with a salary of $250 thousand dollars after taxes, would you take it? Duh! There would just be one catch to it, however. You would just need to be conversant in French in 90 days. Would you do it? I'll bet you would! You would spend the next 90 days studying like never before, and you would learn to speak and understand French.

That is the nature of motivation. It simply means that what we do and how we do it depends on the strength of our motivation doesn't it?

A guy might drag himself out of bed at six o'clock on Monday morning, grumbling, sleepy-eyed, miserable, to go to work. But watch the same man, at the same time in the morning on Saturday, burst out of bed because he and his buddies have a tee-time at the country club. He's wide-eyed, alert, humming a pop tune as he makes coffee and peers out the window to see what the weather is like. It's the same scenario if she is watching for her shopping friends who will be in the crowd as the doors are unlocked at the grand opening of the new Macy's shopping center.

Our reaction in any given situation depends on the cause and how it affects us.

Compare the reaction of a 16 year old lad who has been told that he must mow the lawn, with the reaction of the same lad who has just been sent into the football game with their arch adversary. You would never know he was the same boy. In the first case he looks like a limp sack of indifference from which all interest has been removed; in the second instance, he is a fierce power-house, overcharged with energy.

All right, now examine the way you approach your days.

The reason I say this is because it is a good idea, from time to time, to check and reevaluate your goals. The manner in which we spend our days will depend on what it is that we are working toward. If it is nothing more than graduation, or quitting time, we are not going to be operating on much more than a small fraction of our potential. The bigger and better the target we're shooting for, the more of ourselves we use. And the more of ourselves we use, the more we fulfill ourselves as persons – the happier, the more contented we are.

It always goes back to the goal a person is shooting for. This is the beginning and the end. The bigger the goal, the bigger the person must become to reach it. Oh, my goal? I'd like to earn a comfortable income to support my family of course. In the process I'd like to create a program that allows hundreds, no, thousands of prison convicts to become productive responsible members of society instead of inmates and I would like to allow millions, no, hundreds of millions of government dollars to be spent each year on redemptive programs improving our society rather than housing criminals. That seems like a fairly big goal, don't you agree?

So what are you working toward? Is it worthy of your power? Does it call forth the best that's in you every day? Is it a great and constant vision before your eyes? If so, wonderful! If not, give it some thought. Nothing can bring you peace but you yourself. Self-doubt, hesitation, and confusion stem from the lack of a clear, worthy purpose. Get your purpose right and everything else will fall into place.

You may be sure that there is always a way to everything desirable. What is it that you really want? What is your motivation?" Be your own BFF.

Denny was a bit early. With Perry's help they placed four green field packs, a duffle bag, a large cardboard box and two heavy sport bags in the downstairs closet. The outward appearance of the items suggested that they were not dependent on fragile care. When the closet door was closed, Denny breathed a sigh of relief, but he didn't comment on the contents of the items. He assured Chris that the prospects of a dinner with the family was a treat he had anticipated all day. Sadly, he had to hurry back to Sacramento to catch the last shuttle back to Coronado. The team was being relocated. Chris gave him a tender embrace and thanked him for being such a true friend to Randall.

Chris looked at the clock again. She said to Sue, "I'll bet the phone rings in one minute." The kitchen was quiet for just a couple moments, then burst into laughter as the phone rang. He must have been watching the clock too.

"You're just in time," a delighted Chris said as she answered. "May I open a Shasta Amber for you?"

"Now that is cruel," Randall replied. "Nothing in the world would please me more than to be there in person. I trust Denny accomplished the incidentals?" He wasn't sure how much more of that teasing would be appropriate.

"He was here just long enough to drop off your stuff," she said sweetly. "He said he had to get back to Coronado because the team is moving to D. C. Will you join them next month?"

In a voice of resignation, he replied, "Yeah, if that is where the team will be, I suppose I'll be with them. Since the accident, I've been thinking about my priorities, however. I have about ten months to complete this enlistment. Isn't that about when your Master's will be finished?"

"Hopefully," Chris said softly. "By then I have to make some plans for the future. Julie and I think we would like to live in cool Seattle. I suppose it depends on where I can find a job."

Changing the subject Randall asked, "Did the chaplain get a copy of the Under Construction book to you?"

"Yes, he did and I really liked the introduction," she said brightly. "Would you like to talk about that in the morning. Right now we have a table full of food that needs attention."

"Oh my gosh!" he chuckled. "I lost track of the two hour time difference. Forgive me. Yes let's talk about it in the morning. I'll call you about 0800 your time. It is always a joyful part of my day when we get to chat. Will that work for you?"

Now with a bit of a giggle Chris said, "Roger 1000 your time. Until then try to behave yourself. This is Chico 1, out." They were both laughing out loud.

When the house was quiet for the night Chris tried to clear her mind for sleep, but unfinished conversations interrupted and unspoken questions filled her mind. Finally she turned the light back on and found her notebook. She wrote:

My eyes search an empty sky for the new moon but where can it be?

All I see is darkness from east to west, only twinkling stars beckon me.

But in my heart there is a dawning of celestial promise: I am not alone!

In this night's journey a hidden treasure, hope and joy, rest still as stone.

Hope is the fragile hint of love and joy the glimmer of dynamic faith.

The new moon rises as defenses come down and hearts entwine.

The brilliance of new moon plots a path of faith and fears decline.

Why should I flounder through another minute of moonless night,

When a new moon offers to redeem and restore to a mountain height!

Hope is the fragile hint of love and joy the glimmer of dynamic faith.

He called at 0800. Chico was already a very warm morning and in Dallas it would be another triple digit day. None of that seemed important as they relished in gentle conversation.

"I really enjoyed the story in the introduction to the book," Chris said softly. "That painted a picture of redemption that made sense to me. A young village man had the task of tending the sheep. One day he was caught stealing some of them for himself. He was charged and convicted and his punishment was meant to be a warning to anyone else who might be tempted to make off with a lamb or two. They took a branding iron and printed the letters 'ST', which stood for 'sheep thief', on his forehead for everyone to see.

"When I read that, I thought how all of us have scars from sins others have committed, or we have done to ourselves. A scar is a wound that while healed leaves a lasting mark. Even though this young man had a basically good heart, he was identified as a thief."

"I agree," Randall said softly. "We know he had a good heart because he went to the Lord for forgiveness. He was penitent. I think the story says that he was determined not to be remembered as a thief, so he began helping others and caring for them. He was compassionate and dependable for a long time. In fact he was a model man until he was old and wrinkled, but still the scar could be seen. One day a visitor to the village asked about the meaning of the letters 'ST' on his forehead. Since all those who had convicted and punished him so long ago were no longer present, no one could remember. They suspected it meant 'saint,' because that was what he had become." Neither of them said anything for a moment. They were lost in their own thoughts.

Finally Chris said, "If the rest of this book is as thought provoking, we are going to have a very important six weeks together."

With a bit of a chuckle he added, "I think every moment I get to spend with you is important. The book mentions a poster of a sign that read, 'Be patient with me – God is not finished with me yet.' I like the idea of being under construction. I especially like the idea that we are in this together."

"Me too," Chris agreed. "I just wrote another blog for the alumni newsletter. It was about motivation and nothing can motivate me more, I think, than doing a study with you.

"Let me read the scripture for the first chapter." She opened her Bible to Philippians 3. "We start with these words: *'Not that I have already obtained this or have already reached the goal; but I press on to make it my own, because Christ Jesus has made me his own. Beloved, I do not consider that I have made it my own; but this one thing I do: forgetting what lies behind and straining forward to what lies ahead, I press on toward the goal for the prize of the heavenly call of God in Christ Jesus. Let those of us who are mature be of the same mind; and if you think differently about anything, this too God*

will reveal to you. Only let us hold fast to what we have obtained."
She took a deep breath and said, "That is verses 12 through 16.
What a grand place to begin our conversation about this first
chapter, 'Getting Ourselves Off Our Own Hands'."

Randall's voice was soft as he said, "Thanks for reading
that. Those are familiar words, but hearing you say them
was even more special. I was raised in a perfect home by
perfectionist parents. It is refreshing to hear the contrast of
process instead of perfection." He waited for her response.

"You know a bit of my story," she finally said. "My home
was chaos until I was placed in the shelter home. When I was
14 I started to become a nanny, and of course I was expected
to be perfect at it. But I always considered myself under
construction. I caught the idea of perfection rather than was
taught it by example."

For the rest of the hour they traded accounts of scar making
experiences they had growing up. She heard the timer bell that
Randall had used to keep them from going longer. "I'll call
again at 1900 your time," he said with a sad note. "But I will be
thinking about you every minute until then. Thanks for being
such a great helper. You're a saint."

"It is my pleasure," she said and meant it. "Chico 1, out."
It still made her smile.

The pattern was set for the next six weeks. He called twice
each day and they worked their way through the book:

Week two: When Being Good Is Bad for You;
Week three: Growing in Self Esteem;
Week four: Overcoming the Destructive Don'ts;
Week five: Dealing with Guilt and Shame;
Week six: Getting Ourselves out of Hock;
Week seven: Pay Attention to Yourself.

Then it was September. Time for her to get serious about her thesis and finally time for him to be out of his cast and into a heavy brace.

"It feels like I'm learning to walk all over again," he told her. "The brace is a little stiff, but it holds my knee on track. I'll be comfortable with this in just a few hours." He wanted to assure her, but his larger task was in convincing himself. He could still clearly recall the pain and helplessness as his leg collapsed.

Randall said, "I must be in D.C. by Wednesday afternoon, but do you think I could visit Chico for the weekend before I leave?" He was trembling just like before a battle assignment. He wasn't sure what he would do or say if she declined his request.

"Oh that sounds wonderful," Chris replied happily. "I'll be so glad to see you, and Julie will probably jump to an embarrassing conclusion. Since you and I have spent considerable time together this month, she may think that you're going to be the daddy for her new brother." She would have gone on but he was laughing loudly. When he caught his breath, she continued. "We had a birds and bees sort of discussion because all the other kids have brothers or sisters. She put in her order for a brother, but I tried to explain that it needs a mommy and a daddy for that to happen. She made it clear that I was expected to get with the program." His laughter once again interrupted the conversation. He finally said, "What I was about to suggest is I would get a room at the Ramada Inn near the airport. Then I could drop by two or three times during the long weekend. I would be so glad to take everyone out to dinner one evening at Ernie's Steak House. That place holds nice memories for me."

"Me too," Chris answered in a tender voice. "May I make another suggestion?" She paused for a moment hoping he would be receptive to her offer. "Sue has invited her folks to spend the weekend here. They will be in the downstairs apartment. So the garage apartment will be available if you can manage the stairs. I'm thinking she has an announcement for us. It would be so fun to have you with us the whole time."

"That is so very generous of you," he nearly sang. "I am honored to accept. What can I bring to help?"

"Well let me think." Her voice became hushed and a bit playful. "How about a six pack of Shasta Amber. It has been two years since Bruce's death. We can lift a toast to what brought us together."

"That's a deal for sure," he said with a grin she could nearly see. "I'm getting in about 1500 on Friday. I'll grab a cab and be there in time for happy hour."

"No you won't, sir," she said sternly. "My mama," she tried to make a Texas accent, "told me that hospitality begins with a hug and a kiss. Then you can wet your whistle."

Randall answered, "We sure enough do not want to trouble your mama. I heard she had a cross side that was a sight." He paused, changing the mood from playful to heartfelt. "I'll be counting the hours until I see you."

Softly Chris said with a sigh, "Me too. Chico 1, out."

Sue's folks were a bit concerned about sharing the Labor Day weekend with a stranger, until they learned that he was with Homeland Security stationed in Washington D.C. Then it was an honor to get to know him and learn about his recovery from battle injuries. It was also a privilege to be his guest at Ernie's for supper. Sue and Perry took advantage of the moment to announce that they were, in fact, expecting an Easter baby. Glasses were lifted in happy celebration.

Cupcakes with candles were accompanied by singing "Happy Birthday" for Julie. It made a joyous party time. Before they went home, Chris assured Sue that the golfers would be a chore she could manage for a while so Sue could focus on the delights of motherhood.

At the Saturday barbeque, there was another important

toast. The adults had a bottle of Shasta Amber and Julie had a Crystal Light iced tea as Chris retold the story. "A very large gas bomb was discovered on the roof of the UC admin building. If it had been discovered just a couple hours later the entire school and much of Chico city would have been wiped out." Her voice carried the somber threat of annihilation. "Bruce Meyers, the brave helicopter pilot, landed his aircraft on the roof so that strong men could place the heavy bomb aboard. In a blink he took off for the ocean. The last radio contact they had was he was crossing over the beach and would soon dump the dangerous cargo into the ocean." Her voice took on the hush of a mystery. "We never heard from him again." After a thoughtful moment she raised her glass, saying, "We salute the bravery of Bruce Meyers who defended us all." They drank unaware that the moment was imprinted forever in Julie's heart. Every subsequent Labor Day would become a salute to her heroic father.

A couple hours later, when Julie was tucked in her bed and a noisy pinochle game was happening in the dining room, Randall and Chris sat in the living room reflecting on their successful summer.

"I had excellent care," Randall said, "but I'm convinced it was those hours of conversation with you that gave me the strength to manage the recovery and physical therapy. You were my attending angel."

Chris smiled as she confided, "I calculated that we talked for over 360 hours. I shudder to think about your phone bill."

He took her hand in his and softly said, "Actually, with our new program, it really wasn't that much, but that sort of brings up a subject I need to share with you." Her heart fluttered as she wondered if this was becoming a romantic moment. "I need to explain the items stored in your closet." Silently she thought, "Well that's not even close to romantic."

"Chris, as part of the NSA strike team, it was our duty to

stop drug dealers and destroy their junk," he said seriously. "One part of that junk was piles and piles of money. Michael, our squad leader, believed it was better to confiscate some of that money for a righteous use rather than turning it into ashes. Our instructions were simply to get rid of it." He looked into her eyes and said even more softly, "Downstairs those bags are filled with hundred dollar bills. I have no idea how many or what to do with it. Some of the guys used theirs to buy cars or boats or houses or beach cabins. I've never given it much thought, until now. We agreed there would always be honesty between us." He took a deep breath. "Honestly, I will burn those bags if you think that is the right thing to do."

She recognized that this was a real problem to him. "How much do you guess there might be?" she asked.

He shrugged and said, "The duffle bag must weigh forty or fifty pounds. I've learned that a bill weighs one gram, which means that a pound of one hundreds equals forty five thousand four hundred dollars. I would guess in all there has to be at least fifty million dollars."

The enormity of what he was telling her began to sink in. "And how many bags are there?" she asked.

"They were collected as we were setting explosives to destroy everything. It was either save it or destroy it, which seemed a terrible waste." He added, trying to help her understand the urgency at the time of collection. "The four field packs were the first. Then Michael started using his duffle bag which is three times larger. So I did too. The box must be at least as large as three field packs and the sport bags are as large as four. Each bag represents a successful mission. The two sport bags were from the final one where I was injured." He was quiet for a moment. "But you asked how many bags. Seven bags and a box. Your guess is as good as mine on how many dollars they hold; enough for a very noble endeavor or comfortable retirement even if we started today."

She squeezed his hand and said, "You trust me enough

to tell me about it. I can sort of understand your dilemma, especially if your command leader started and approved it. You have it but can't bank it or spend much of it without setting off IRS alarms, but you can donate to Second Chance as soon as I get a nonprofit registration." She was still for a moment, then added, "My admiration for you has just increased now that I know you are rich as well as so darned handsome."

Randall was silent for a moment before whispering; "Now you have taken the high road for me. I don't need to tell you how endearing that is." He moved beside her and embraced her tenderly, kissing her hair.

Chris softly said, "If God can redeem us for a special purpose, why can't those dollars be redeemed in the same way? They are not ill-gotten gain or stolen." She turned her face toward him so they could share a gentle kiss, something they had both wished could happen for a long time. The room was rosy still. That kiss sort of scrambled her thoughts. "Mmm, that was as nice as I imagined it would be," she purred. "Now what were we talking about? Oh yeah, millions of dollars. Would you mind if I help with it? Officially it will be fringe legal, but I do believe there might be a redemptive way to use the golfers as a shield of some sort." She snuggled against his neck. "We can find a way to redeem those dollars back into circulation," is what she said, but the warmth of that kiss is what she was more thrilled about.

Sunday morning was leisurely with Chris preparing her famous French toast cream cheese casserole with scrambled eggs and bacon. Julie admitted she had never tasted any breakfast better. The adults smiled knowing that she had a very limited range of examples to compare, but it went well with the relaxed morning. Perry suggested that afterward the folks might enjoy a countryside tour of the farm land and fruit stands around Chico. He said that he knew of one that was even a petting corral of goats and welcomed Julie to come along if she would like. Chris grinned knowing that he was only making possible a couple hours for her to be alone with Randall.

They sat at the kitchen table, holding hands across the corner. She asked him about his flight schedule in the morning. He asked if he could visit again in December. She told him about her final round of class sessions and thesis presentation. He told her about the probability of some sort of leg brace for at least the foreseeable future. Finally after a lengthy silence, he asked her the question that had been on both their minds.

"Chris Honey, I've been afraid to ask you about the future. I've been so uneasy about my D.C. posting and your future. Neither of us knows what to expect. May I ask you a very serious question?" He drew in a long breath.

Chris was quiet for a moment then answered, "I've been afraid you weren't going to do that. We have talked about a lot of important things. My heart knows there is one that we both want to talk about but don't know how to start." Her smile was brave if not confident.

"I hope I understand what you are suggesting," he said softly. "Because my heart knows where I want to spend my future; right with you, wherever that may be. I would love to be married to you. Am I correct in thinking that you may be feeling the same way?"

Shyly Chris looked down for a moment and then met his steady gaze. "I've been most afraid that you would leave without having this conversation. Yes, I very much welcome that plan and so want to be your wife. All those hours of conversation as you were in reconstruction," she wrinkled her nose playfully, "and the information that we shared with one another has made you a permanent part of my heart. I want to share our future with you as well." She paused and then reminded him, "That includes Julie. She thinks of you as a member of our family already."

With a large smile he asked, "Would you like to wait until

next summer for a wedding, or do you prefer a Christmas wedding in just four months?"

She came around the table so she could kiss him. "I can't think of one reason why we should wait until school is out or you are separated from the Corps. I am thrilled to anticipate a Christmas wedding, even if it means there will be some times when we are apart. Being married to you is my top priority. Everything else is just commentary and incidentals. You know," she sort of thought out loud, "my brother in Seattle has a large home and conducts weddings there. Would a very low key service be disappointing to you?" She looked into his pleasant gaze.

"Not if that's your preference," he said happily. "In fact that sounds very sweet. I've wondered if you would like to have Chaplain White do the honors since he has been a special support to you for the past four or five years"

She was still for a moment then said softly, "I am charmed again and again by the fact that you look out for my feelings so tenderly." She kissed him and asked, "What do you think of the idea of saying the dinner blessing this evening and asking for God's blessing on our marriage as well? I think that would be an attention grabber." Her eyes sparkled joyfully. The house would be a busy place tonight; there was much to talk about.

Heads were bowed as the blessing prayer was being spoken. "And Lord we remember to give you thanks and praise for the abundance of your grace, for the food before us, the hospitality that presents it. We give you thanks for the love that abides here and especially ask your blessing on the up-coming marriage. May we in all ways reflect the joy and peace you have displayed in the one called Jesus. It is in his name we pray, Amen." The heads were no longer bowed and everyone was exclaiming surprise, especially Julie.

Randall's beaming smile was a clue that something special was happening. He came around the table to stand before

Chris. "I would kneel, Love, but it would take two strong backs to help me up." He opened his hand to reveal a small black box. Everyone recognized a ring box. He opened it revealing a gorgeous engagement ring.

"Chris, will you bless me by becoming my wife? I believe together we will discover God's amazing plan for our lives."

She rose to accept the ring and embraced him. After a sweet kiss she said, "I am so delighted to say, 'yes' I want to walk beside you always." There was another kiss while the folks at the table applauded.

Randall turned toward Julie and from his pocket produced a very small gold ring with a pink stone. When he took her hand the delighted child burst out, "I get one too! We are a married family!"

He said softly, "Julie will you be my daughter? I would be honored to love and protect you as a father should." He bent down so he could give her a gentle embrace. Tears and a firm head nod were her positive answers.

After a few moments of happy response, Chris explained their introduction, courtship and marvelous assurance which grew out of hours and hours of conversation. "We probably know more about each other than our parents do. Yes, we are delighted to be able to announce our marriage plans. You are the first to hear about it. We'll work out the details later." The house was indeed busy with excited conversation for the rest of the evening.

The morning was just dawning when he came into the kitchen to say goodbye. He found Chris had prepared a hardy breakfast for them to share. "I know you could have had a sandwich later, but I want to remind you again and again how much I want to care for you." There were kisses that flavored the food. But finally she drove him to the airport and knew that one more kiss would have to last for three months. She pressed against him and knew that he would miss her as much as she would miss him. She watched as he limped into the terminal, then the tears were released. But they were happy tears that were confident of the future.

Tuesday morning she was still joyfully aware of their new affection. She was also aware of a different way to express her involvement, however, with the beginning of her strategy. She would find out if her plan would work. It began at Sierra National Bank. "Good morning Mr. Steinman, yes the golfers are already here and grateful for our sunny weather. Do you have enough time for a practical question?" When he invited her to have a seat in his office she continued, "Your predecessor explained to me why we have this three day verification of funds from a foreign source. Some of the time that works smoothly. But times like this when we have a Monday holiday, we get behind a day. Mr. Edward, the agent in Kyoto, has asked if it would be easier for you if our deposit could be in the form of cash rather than a troublesome draft. It really makes no difference to us. But it would be more efficient if you didn't need to make that over-night contact with his bank. On the other hand, I suppose counting all that cash would take time as well." She couldn't read his expression so she had no idea if her suggestion was being considered.

"If I recall," he began, "you have as many as a hundred and fifty tourists who are here to simply play golf for four days. Is that correct?" His tone of voice was not very accommodating.

"That is correct sir," Chris said lightly. "The success of the program may even add an additional 70, which would make a deposit of nearly nine hundred thousand dollars. There is a group each and every week, so it may be asking too much for someone to count all that cash."

Karl Steinman, the new branch director was thinking about the daily report that would show a significant increase in currency volume rather than an electronic exchange. It would make an apparent positive increase since his arrival.

"Oh I think the folks could handle that extra work for you. It would help if you could be here when we open at ten o'clock and make sure you always go to the commercial teller." It seemed that was all the conversation she was going to receive so she thanked him and only smiled in satisfaction as she made out a deposit slip.

"Oh my," the teller whispered. "You'll have to bring that into the work room." She opened the security door and led Chris into another locked space. There she made several stacks of one hundred dollar bills and started running them through the counter machine. In only a couple minutes she asked, "Does six thousand match your count? That's a deposit of six hundred thousand dollars."

"Yes it does," Chris smiled with satisfaction, "And I did it twice to make sure." She then explained to the teller how the cash was to be used. "We have a pretty constant supply of Japanese golfers. I'll be back next Monday with another case full." The first step had been as easy as she had hoped.

Her next stop was the Cornerstone Federal Bank in the East Hills Shopping center. As she entered she was aware of the differences in this suburban facility. It was much smaller with fewer staff. But the manager was immediately recognized by her warm smile. "Mrs. Meyers, it's good to see you again. How can I help you?" Carry Gomez was the former manager of the Sierra bank.

"I heard you made a move, Chris said brightly and I must admit I've had some trouble with deposits written on a Japanese bank. You didn't seem to mind the three day lag. I wonder if I can transfer part of my account here. It would only be the golfer's money and some thirty year Treasuries occasionally from the left-over's. But at least we would get to greet one another from time to time."

Mrs. Gomez's gentle smile hid the satisfaction of hearing that the man who replaced her was losing a valued customer. She was also aware that even a portion of the volume of business the golfers brought would be a significant increase for her small bank. "Have a seat and let's get you going with a new account."

After the information was exchanged and the golfer's check was deposited, Chris said, "You may recall that two years ago my husband was killed in a helicopter accident." Mrs. Gomez nodded. "I've been receiving annuity payments that have just been sitting in my account there. What would you think about turning some of that into Treasuries?"

The banker could not hide the look of satisfaction. Not only was Steinman losing the golfer business, he was missing out on some real money makers. Treasuries were cash cows deluxe! "I think that would be a splendid idea for you. They earn interest and are very safe investments. Just let me know a bit in advance how many you might need."

Chris asked, "And does this branch have safety deposit boxes where I can hold those treasuries?"

"Oh of course," Mrs. Gomez assured her. "We are a small branch but a full service bank to care for you."

Chris offered her handshake saying, "Do you think I could start with twenty next week?" Carry's handshake became more vigorous as she answered, "Definitely! I'll be happy to take care of that for you."

Chris's cheery smile was authentic because she was so pleased with the ease of this transaction. Now if the following weeks would work as well. "It is so good to see you again, Carry. I'm glad you had time to help me today. I'll see you next week and we can do it again." That process continued for nine months during which she was able to redeem thirty four million dollars into Treasuries. At the same time she had been over depositing each week at the Sierra bank and had an additional deposit box with seven hundred more Treasuries.

The director of the Master's thesis was Dr. J. Wahdoni who studied her folder carefully. "Miss Meyers, this is a well thought-out proposal. I think if you spend a bit more time on support recommendations for the first and second phases and develop a plan for fund raising, this will be a very competent thesis. Do you know what you will do with it?"

Chris's smile conveyed her satisfaction in this initial presentation. She had carefully supported each element of her Second Chance concept with academic studies and references. Additional information would be an easy add-on. "Right now it is only conceptual," she said with a happy smile. "But I have had interest from the state DSHS office. They think I may fit in one of several open director situations."

Dr. Wahdoni tapped the neat stack of paper with his pencil. "Well I think it merits a wider exposure," he affirmed. "May I suggest that you send a copy to HR of both Nevada and Arizona? While you're at it, how about Oregon and Washington too? Someone with vision and deep pockets will be more than interested I will wager. If that happens I will be able to move this from a concept file to an active design. That would be a hop and a skip from a doctorate if you are interested." His warm smile implied she should at least think about it.

"I'm not sure what I am going to do with an MBA," Chris said brightly, "let alone a doctorate. I certainly don't feel drawn to teaching. But I will think about it."

At seven o'clock precisely Randall called. Chris's happy grin reflected the understanding that he had waited until 10 p.m. his time, for their evening chat. "What a guy!" she thought. He was eager to hear about her conversation with Wahdoni and her two final classes. She was eager to hear about his doctor's assessment of the healing process on his injury and the prognosis. She also asked about his desk job in D.C. He asked about Julie's first days in kindergarten and she asked when he could take a long weekend to spend in Chico. A pleasant hour of conversation was the best part of their day. Before the call ended, Randall mentioned that he had been scouring the GSA (General Services Administration) bulletins for government properties being auctioned as surplus. "I'm emailing information on a half dozen possible candidates for Second Chance," he told her. "If any of them look promising, I'll see if I may join you for an inspection. The date and place of the auction is on the bottom of the page. I miss you more with every breath."

"I love you too, you big hunk, a hunk a burnin' love." She giggled at her own playfulness. "Now you have given me motivation to carefully study those properties if there is a chance I would get to see you sooner." They chatted until she heard the timer he had set for an hour. With a tender goodnight, he promised to call again tomorrow night.

September scurried by with the Chico house routine running smoothly. Sue's gratitude was frequently expressed as Chris continued to look after the golfers and did most of the shopping and cooking too. Morning sickness was eased as the expectant mom could get extra bed rest. Chris explained that if she didn't stay real busy she would probably explode with eagerness to see Randall again.

The second Monday of October the stars must have been in line or something unusual, because Chris had four calendar requests. At breakfast, Perry asked if there were any Thanksgiving plans. When he was told there were none to Chris's knowledge, he said he would love to invite his folks from Iowa for the weekend. Within the hour Dr. J. Wahdoni requested an afternoon meeting with Chris. "I have very good news for you," was his only clue. Before lunch Gram Holly called to invite Chris and Julie to Seattle for a few Thanksgiving days. Just after lunch a lady from the Washington State HR called to tell Chris that the registrar had informed them that an MBA graduate was available and there were three attractive administrative jobs open if she would be interested. Finally, Randall called to tell her that he had located a very interesting surplus property that was formerly a Canadian Army officer's quarters. His voice sort of rose in pitch as he said, "It's situated on twenty seven acres of view hillside just across the river from Portland. If we could get it and divide the land into lots, we could make a killing!" he said.

"Rans," she said as sweetly as possible, "With seven bags of cash in the closet, what would we do with more?"

"Oh yeah," he answered thoughtfully. "I sort of forgot about that situation. But this really does look like a plum for picking."

Chris said teasingly, "Sweetie, you can tell me the truth. You miss me and just wanted to hear my voice, huh?"

He could tell she was nearly giggling. "When and where is the auction?" She felt his enthusiasm deserved a friendly response whatever the reason.

"It's going to be sold to the highest bidder Tuesday November 21st at 1300. One of the conditions is financing must be in place to successfully bid. I thought we could have a field pack available." Now she knew he was smiling. "You and Julie could meet me in Portland. I know they have a big Zoo." Now he was just spreading it on.

Softly Chris said, "Rans, I didn't understand that you were so sold on the concept of Second Chance." Her voice had turned more serious. "Do you really believe it could work?"

He matched her serious mood. "I think it was inspired to help both our prison system and the folks who are in it with little chance for redemption." He paused before saying more boldly, "Yeah, I think it deserves a shot."

"Then let me tell you about my busy morning. First I learned that the faculty committee met on my behalf and determined that I have satisfied all requirements for my MBA. Dr. J. Wahdoni has spoken with all my instructors and knows that even if I crash and burn on the final three papers and a test, I will still have a prominent grade point. A lady from Olympia Washington has asked me to consider some job opening she has, one of which is supervisor of a group of women's shelters.

Her name is Ruth Justin and she is very interested in my thesis project as well. On top of that, Gram Holly has invited us to share Thanksgiving with them in Shoreline, just north of Seattle. Their son Carter, who is also in the Corps, will be there with his family. So if you fly into Seattle on Monday, we could get a couple rooms at the Silver Cloud. That's where Julie and I stayed last Christmas. Then we could say hello to the family and on Tuesday morning Julie could stay with them and we could get down to Vancouver in a couple of hours. That would give us plenty of time to kick the tires and scope out the rest of the property. How does that sound?"

"Any plan that lets me spend an extra day with you girls is a winner with me." he said happily. "I'll get a rental car if you will drive. The doc hasn't given me clearance to operate machinery or fire my side-arm."

The visit started well as Randall was introduced to the Windsor's. Handshakes all around were interrupted when he came to Carter who was casually dressed. The younger man stood erect and said, "I'm honored to meet you, sir. I'm Staff Sergeant Carter Windsor, Data Processing west."

"At ease, Windsor. We are all only family here. I am happy to be your brother." He allowed that to have a double meaning and he noticed Chris's delighted smile.

Brightly, Cindy asked, "Are you two.." both Carter and Chris held their breath dreading the rest of the question. … "skiers by any chance? There has been an early snowfall and Crystal Mountain is already opening." She couldn't understand why there was so much laughter, until Randall turned to show her the metal brace he was still wearing.

The young woman murmured, "Oh, I forgot about that. It might be difficult, huh?"

For the following four or five hours there was happy family chatter and the enjoyment of including the Gunnery Sergeant into the growing family circle. It was most surprising to Carter that after service in several foreign countries, his near fatal injury had been in domestic interdiction. The fact that the clandestine nature of the battle was confidential made it even more fascinating. Randall was grateful for the announcement that the barbeque was ready and the subject would change. Gram Holly was a model hostess until it was bedtime for exhausted children. Then Chris explained that they were also in Washington to inspect a potential piece of property in Orchards. So Holly extended her hospitality by inviting them to a modest breakfast in the morning.

That plan worked marvelously. Perhaps Julie was the happiest because Gram Holly said that the cousins could visit the bookstore for more fun stories.

"Is this a freeway?" Randall asked. "It seems like a pretty crowded street." They were approaching the down town part of Seattle along with a crowd of folks anxious to get to work.

"This is Aurora Avenue southbound, old highway 99, which would take us right to Chico," Chris said brightly. "Of course that would take two very long days. We are running parallel to I-5 south. Holly said this would have less traffic this time of the day. We'll join I-5 near the airport." She wanted to talk about their purpose of this trip. "What do you expect to find in Orchards?" They had read the description and studied the photo. "This seems like a pretty long drive just on a hunch." Her smile assured him there was nothing critical implied.

His grin was almost playful. "Any excuse that gets me out of D.C. and with you is worth it. But more than that, I have been impressed with your concept. It feels to me that this could be a huge change-maker. It could change so many lives and a prison system that is antiquated at best." He chuckled in that way she loved. "When I saw the photo and heard the address, officer's quarters for Fort Vancouver in Orchards, this one seemed different from all the others we had seen."

"You're right," she said as she reached for his hand and

gave him a happy squeeze. "Any excuse that allows us to be together for a few days is worth the effort."

They passed through a short tunnel and emerged on an elevated roadway that ran parallel to the waterfront. "Oh wow!" he exclaimed. "This is neat. It feels like a miniature Fishermen's Wharf in San Francisco."

"Yeah," she sounded like a tour guide, "this was the active departure point for the nineteenth century Alaska gold rush. Do you see how all the docks are angled? They had train tracks to move lots of building materials and miners."

"Look at those snowy mountains across the bay!" he marveled.

She explained a bit of the geography of the Olympic Peninsula that she could remember.

"I didn't know Seattle was set in all this beauty." Craning around to see more he continued his interest, "And you say this is tidal ocean water?"

Chris found herself joining his enthusiasm and appreciation for what had been overly familiar to her. Randall was delighted with Tacoma, another waterfront city. Fort Lewis and McCord air field were appreciated, but not as much as Mt. Rainier and then the remnant of Mt. Saint Helens. A glimpse of the state capitol and then the mighty Columbia River indicated they were close to their destination. A road sign announced a rest area and Randall suggested a stop to stretch his legs would be welcome. Several other travelers recognized both his camos and heavy brace. They went out of their way to greet him and shake his hand. One grey haired man said it was too early in the day but offered him a twenty dollar bill saying, "I'd like to buy you a beer later. Thanks for your service."

When they were back on the freeway, he studied the money and laughed softly saying, "I can't remember a morning any better than this. This is just great!"

GPS advised her to turn onto highway I-205, which would bypass Portland if they were going that far. Instead it guided them to the Orchards address and a very rundown three story building situated between the Fort Vancouver State Park and the Union Pacific Railroad yard. A fellow was just closing the door as they pulled up. He waited politely until Randall was out of the car, then he asked, "Are you Howe, or Tran by any chance?" Randall carefully made his way across the uneven dirt to him and offering his hand said, "I'm Randall Howe. I'm the one who contacted you about the auction. This is my fiancée Chris Myers.

As the man shook her hand he identified himself. "Good morning. I'm Kenny Fox from Multnomah Construction. I was asked to evaluate this old building." His smile grew as he asked Chris, "Forgive me for staring. Have we met before? You seem very familiar to me."

Her buoyant mood was still at work. "No, I believe I would remember a courteous man named Fox. I don't believe our paths have crossed."

"Let me make a quick call, and then I can show you through the building." He was gone just a couple minutes. "Now then, before I get into a lengthy history lesson, can you tell me what your interest in this old shamble might be? We have only one other interested party and he wants to tear it down and subdivide the property for a housing development. Is your interest along those lines?" His gentle smile was only reflecting a remote interest.

Randall answered before Chris as he pointed to the railroad yard just to the east side of the property. "If I were going to develop a residential place, I would not want it near a noisy bunch of stinky diesel engines."

Chris answered more positively, "I just finished my MBA at UC Chico. My thesis is a proposal to replace a certain element of our state penitentiary system that seems harsh and antiquated. I would like to build a more productive and efficient test model."

"Wow! That sounds interesting," he said. "Would you excuse me for just another minute? I need to call my office again."

When he returned he asked, "Well now; where should we begin? There is a bad place and then there is a really bad one. My friend often says if you have to swallow a frog, don't look at it too long. And if you have to swallow two frogs, take the big one first." He chuckled at the gross idea but Randall recalled that he had often heard Michael say that same thing. The contractor said, "I had the power turned on for today, so let's go into the basement first."

After a few minutes, Chris said, "Mr. Fox, it is not necessary to show us any more. I get the idea. Everything must be torn out and replaced. It needs a new foundation as well as a new roof. So tell me, can this old girl be made new again? Can you give me an estimate of the restoration?"

Kenny smiled because she sounded and even thought just like him. "I can tell you that a basic renovation could be done for a hundred thousand dollars. To make an impressive test model of what I think you would be happy to show could be that much again. This is a little premature to make a bid, however."

The men saw that gracious smile that touched their hearts. "It gives me an idea of what a dream might cost," Chris said softly. "There are castles in air and then there is practicality. I think we can get them pretty close, don't you agree?" Both men were nodding agreement. "There are just an awful lot of priorities right now. This is high on my list, but there is also a wedding next month, a house in Chico to sell and a new home somewhere in Washington to find. I'm not sure if I will look for a job before or after all that fun stuff." She was charming in playful reflection.

Kenny looked at his watch and said, "It's almost lunchtime

and the Chart House is only a few blocks from here. Would you like to follow me if I promise to pick up the tab?" Randall was nodding.

On the way Randall turned toward Chris and asked with an over-large smile, "Are you as thrilled with the possibility as I think you are?"

"I wasn't at first," she answered after a bit of thought. "In fact I was only trying to be courteous. But he seems like such a nice guy. Do you think he was being serious about knowing me before?"

"Yeah I think he was sincere. That wasn't some trick line." He was quiet for a moment then added, "For an important auction to be happening in just a couple hours, he seems pretty casual though. I wish I knew everything that is happening right now."

There were only a few cars parked in front of the Chart House. One of them was a limo.

In the lobby an attractive lady was waiting. She wore a stylish black dress and a bit of a smile. She seemed to be waiting for them because she greeted Kenny and then turned toward Chris. As her hand held Chris's she said, "Oh yes, I see. I'm very happy to meet you, Chris." Turning to Randall she said, "And you, sir, must be our contact who has made this meeting possible. Kenny tells me you are a brave warrior." Her hand held his a bit longer just as she had held Chris's. "Yes, I see," she said softly. "It is an honor and a wonderful pleasure to meet you both."

Kenny explained, "Miss Chambers is the attorney representing the Canadian holding firm that owns the property. She was eager to meet you and answer any questions you might have about it."

As they were being seated near a window overlooking the Columbia River and on the far side of it the Portland airport, Miss Chambers noticed Randall check his watch. She smiled and said softly, "If you are worried about the time of the auction, I should tell you that it has been cancelled. A poster is being placed on the front door advising any walk-in bidders that the property is being held by the EPA until contamination can be removed from the soil. That was the story that Mr. Tran heard and accepted. So you see we have a longer lunchtime." Chris thought she was a mysterious woman and Randall thought she was super attractive with a lot of information that she was not sharing. He was suspicious of people who were secretive.

Her friendly brown eyes studied him for a moment before asking, "How is your wound coming along, Mr. Howe? That doesn't seem like a middle east sort of injury."

He felt like she knew more than he had mentioned so he said simply, "It's improving every day. Torn tendons and arteries heal slowly, but praise God they do heal."

"Yes. We are happy that your future seems very bright." Her gaze shifted to Chris. "And you young lady have a concept that might impact the criminal justice world." Chris was about to speak to the over-statement but Miss Chambers said, "Tell us about your family."

Chris felt an unusual kindness toward a question that could have been too prying. "There's very little to tell" she said quietly. "My family disintegrated when I was about six. My dad and older brother moved to a different town. I never saw them again. Mom had a problem and soon my little brother was in a foster home and I was in a shelter home for abused girls. In high school I got a job as a nanny and after graduation moved to Chico as a nanny and student. Two horrible violent moments left me as a widow and foster mother of a six year old daughter. We are making the best of a new start." She gave Randall's arm a happy pat.

There was honest admiration in Miss Chambers' smile as she said, "Oh my goodness, for one so young to experience such turmoil and anguish, yet you have managed to hold fast to the high ground with a sweet positive disposition. I'll bet this warrior," she nodded toward Randall, "is delighted to have such a stalwart future spouse.

Chris replied, "We both feel blessed by the crazy chain of events that has brought us together. The best part is that he loves Julie, my daughter, and she adores him."

"Before our food comes," Miss Chambers said in a hushed voice, "let me say that the opening bid on the property here was going to be one hundred thousand dollars. That is what the tax assessor believes is the value of just the twenty seven acres. If you are interested in making your model here I will accept that as your winning bid. I would so enjoy having you as a friend in this metro area." There was that smile that just tugged at her heart.

Randall leaned toward her and said, "We are happy to accept that offer. Just give me your contact information and I will take care of the finances."

Miss Chambers slid a card to him as though it had been all ready to go. Yes she was a mystifying woman.

A marvelous lunch was enjoyed as they chatted about the history of the property and the beauty of the area, even on such an overcast day. Finally they walked Miss Chambers out to the limo, promising to see her again. Randall was ready to get in their car and head north when Kenny made a surprise offer.

"I was at the property this morning only because I have been asked by Wells Fargo to appraise the damage in a house they have as a foreclosure. A young couple bought a lovely home just up the hill. They were on a cruise when a group of college kids broke in and for over a week rained havoc on the place. The damage is unbelievable. The couple couldn't afford to make repairs even after an insurance settlement and the bank took the place back. They have hired me to do the clean up and repairs, but they really want to just get rid of it. I know that you didn't come here today looking for a home. But if you are selling the Chico house to relocate somewhere in this area, I feel that this might be one of those serendipity moments. Would you like to see it?" His happy eyes searched Chris's then Randall's.

The man in camos said, "It's not even time for the auction yet. We've had great luck so far today, what do we have to lose?" Chris happily nodded in agreement.

The residential area they turned into was prominent and quiet. The houses were set back further from the street with extra large properties of at least an acre each. Some had gates and many had walls. In the second block they came to one that had yellow police crime tape marking it as a no trespassing driveway. Kenny removed the tape and they gathered at a remarkable one story home with several broken windows. The front doors had been smashed and the attractive porch lights were hanging shattered as well.

Kenny said, "When we go in try not to see the damage and destruction, but look at the layout of the rooms and imagine how gracious it will be when we get it restored. We can redeem this beauty." He was speaking more excitedly without knowing that he was using trigger words that were from the couple's long summer study.

As they stepped through the broken door Kenny pointed out a library and coat closet on one side and an office of sorts on the other that formed an entryway. Kenny gave the general information about the place, saying, "There is nearly four thousand square feet on this level and the same in a daylight basement. We didn't see the three car garage at the end of this hall. There are two bedrooms that share a large bathroom on one side of this hallway and a laundry and a guest bathroom on the other side." Pointing to the other hallway he said, "That one has a huge media room on the front side and the most gorgeous master suite you can imagine with a glass wall that looks at the river and Mt. Hood. The dining and living area sort of blend in an open concept. The kitchen is better than most commercial designs. There is a kitchen table area…" He would have described more but Randall raised his hand.

"I believe we are not alone in here," he said softly. "It would be a good idea to call the police. If someone is hiding downstairs they may feel trapped and desperate."

Kenny whispered, "I didn't hear anything. Are you sure that there is someone there?"

The trio was very still for a moment, and then Randall said, "I believe there are two. One might be a woman."

Kenny called 911. Almost immediately he was speaking to a watch commander who advised them to leave the building immediately. A dispatched car would be there in six minutes.

Randall shook his head. "In six minutes we will lose the advantage and all the information they have for us," he said quietly. "You two stay up here. I'll look around downstairs." He headed for the large stairway.

"Oh no you don't," Chris said as she followed him. "You are in no condition to be gallant." Kenny was hurrying to catch up. This was not what he had in mind for a home inspection.

There was plenty of natural light in the large activity room that was strewn with debris; a pile of broken furniture was stacked against the wall. Fortunately Kenny had a strong flashlight that immediately lit up the hallway that Randall had just entered. The contractor said in a hushed voice, "Randall, wait! The police are on their way. They can handle it." He had said enough to be heard by those hiding in the darkness.

At the far end of the hall a face came out of a side room; it belonged to a rumpled young man carrying a table leg as a club. He shouted, "Out of my way Slim; I don't want to hurt you!" His bold stride quickened as he rushed at Randall.

To Chris the drama was happening too fast. She was frozen in place. Kenny didn't know what he should do so he just kept the light shining down the hall. The trespasser was desperate and obviously not familiar with combat. He may have even closed his eyes as he began to swing the club. To Randall the action was in slow motion. He had placed himself in the center of the hall leaving room on either side for avoidance. When he saw the blow begin he simply dodged down to the right side, and as the club went over his head he sprang forward with a fist trained to do damage. The young man was unconscious before he crashed to the floor with a broken jaw.

The hallway was still lighted by Kenny's flashlight but now it was trembling. The sound of sirens interrupted the stillness until a voice from the back room called out, "Please don't hurt me! I surrender, don't hit me."

A smaller rumpled young man emerged into the light with his hands raised and immediately saw his fallen comrade lying motionless. "Is Sean dead? Please don't hurt me! I can give you the names of the people who did the damage! Please don't hurt me." Kneeling beside his semi-conscious buddy he was weeping as three policemen hurried down the stairs.

"Hey, Gus, it's Kenny Fox from Multnomah Construction. I just brought a couple in who might be interested in fixing this place up." The police officers each had a flashlight and the hallway was now flooded with light. "This is Gunnery Sergeant Howe and his lady Chris Meyers."

One of the officers pointed to the table leg asking, "Did you use that to subdue him?"

Before Randall could answer, Kenny said, "The trespasser tried to strike the Sergeant with that. It was self defense."

The officer in charge stepped between them and introduced himself. "I'm watch officer Gus Crain, the one you spoke with. We'll take over from here. Thank you for your service, sir. If we need a statement from you we'll call you into the station."

Randall smiled and said, "As long as you understand that Miss Meyers lives in Chico California and I'm stationed with Homeland in D.C."

Once again Kenny spoke up. "I will be glad to make a statement when you need it Gus. These folks are on their way back to Seattle this afternoon." Handcuffs were being securely attached to a young man who was still weeping and one who was moaning in pain.

They were ready to get into their car when Kenny asked, "We couldn't see its best features, but what do you think about this opportunity?"

Randall shook the contractor's hand, telling him what a memorable day this had been. "I know that a short sale can be a lengthy process. If the numbers are right we are very interested, but it just depends on the numbers. I seem to recall that you said it was a Wells Fargo Bank that is involved. It just so happens that I have an account with those folks." For the past two years he had been quietly moving some of that confiscated money into a number of his accounts. "If the price is right, you may pass along the information that I can transfer the full amount to them." He gave Kenny a business card with his contact information. "We'll be in Seattle until Sunday. We both must get back to work."

Chris was very quiet for the first few miles of their return north. She did ask if he would like a rest stop. As soon as they were back on the freeway, Randall asked, "Why so quiet, sweet lady? Are you upset with me?"

Chris took a deep breath to calm her emotions and said, "I just don't understand why you went downstairs into danger when you are still healing from your last encounter. You knew the police were on their way to take care of it. Are you just fond of knocking people around?" She clamped her lips tight before she said more, but she did anyway. Softly she said, "Or did you think that in some way we were in danger and you were protecting us?" She took a deep breath. "I felt sorry for that young man. His jaw was really messed up." She glanced at him and added, "There was so much that happened this morning. It was so much more than I was expecting both good and bad. I thought you would want to talk, you know check in with one another. There were lots of questions rattling around in my head about acquiring either or both of those properties. Then out of the blue you just sealed the deal. That puzzled me." She was thoughtful for a long moment. "I guess I feel a little left out of the decision-making process. I thought this was something we were going to do together." Her voice had a bit of a tremor.

"Oh Sweetness," he said as he tried to twist as far toward her as he could. "The very last thing I intended this morning was to offend you. I am so very sorry. I do not welcome conflict of any sort. For the last decade, however, I have been very well trained to stabilize a situation. I used just enough force to control the moment." Now it was his turn to quietly collect his thought. With a very subdued voice he said, "Perhaps this is a new lesson time for me. If I could be a more gentle person you would not be confused about me. I need to learn from your gentleness or kindness. I have dreamed of being a team with you in every way. For sure I don't want you to feel left out of any part of this day. Will you forgive me?"

Chris thought for a moment and concluded, "Perhaps we can teach each other a number of valuable lessons. I've always thought I was a bit of a pansy. Yes, I forgive you."

Now Randall tried to clarify by speaking more boldly, "We are going to talk hours about a lot of things including both of those places. We are going to talk about their use, their finish, their color, everything." Now it was his turn to choose his words carefully. "What would you say if I told you that our activity today has insured Julie's college education? That's about what our net worth has increased today. If you want to fix up the old officer's quarters that's a decision we can make later. The same thing is true with that house. We didn't get to see all of it, but that's not important. If we can get it on a foreclosure sale and Kenny can doll it up, our net worth will increase another half million dollars. That surely doesn't mean that we won't talk about it. There are endless conversations including how many children we want to raise in it. I just didn't want to miss the opportunity to acquire them both. Does that sound more reasonable?"

Chris nodded and tried a smile that didn't quite convince him.

He said more softly, "I never want to cause you to feel left out. If we don't want to use the officer's quarters, we will sell it at a sweet profit. If we don't want to live in the Orchard house, we will either sell it or I will add it to my leased fleet. For the last three years I have acquired some rentals. There are three commercial properties and four homes in Richardson, Texas that are being managed by a firm there. The six houses I was able to get on Coronado Island are also leased by a management firm. It was a way I could redeem some of the early money."

Now her smile became one of surprise. "You have ten houses?" she asked in wonder.

"Yes," he said with a nod, "and three commercial warehouses. I try not to think about them, but every year I get a report that tells me they are still making money the real way."

Chris said, "In all those hours of conversation last summer, you never thought to mention ten houses?" Her tone was surprise and not accusation.

He shook his head and softly said, "I don't think of them very often, sort of like my back left pocket."

"What?" she asked a bit bewildered? "What does your pocket have to do with anything?"

With a grin he said, "That's just it. We don't think about that pocket because it doesn't have much use, just like the ten houses."

His satisfied smile was incongruous but endearing. Finally she began to smile too. He felt that his nonsense was an explanation of sorts. The more she thought about it the more silly it became. With a bit of a disgusted chuckle she said, "Men!" She drove in silence for a few minutes and then said firmly, "But I still want to talk a lot about both the officer's place and that wonderful house! Don't you think that could be the most interesting place you've ever lived?"

"Sweetheart," Randall said warmly, "wherever you are is the most interesting place. I want to talk a lot about that too and I want to learn how to be gentle."

By the time they got back to Seattle they had talked positively about both opportunities and there were two emails waiting for them. The one from Miss Chambers was a Purchase and Sales Agreement that they could sign and fax back. It also had information for transferring funds. The one from Kenny invited them back Friday morning. The bank had agreed immediately to his proposal and the price was enticingly fair. Papers could be signed and funds transferred. It would take a bit of time to process everything. But it would happen after several hours of conversation.

The Thanksgiving visitors had different flights scheduled for early Sunday afternoon. Completing her fabulous hospitality, Gram Holly prepared a delicious brunch for them. It was a time of farewells, of gratitude for gracious hospitality and a growing appreciation for new family.

Quietly Cindy said, "Chris, I am so thrilled about your successful MBA. Do you think you will accept one of those DHSH positions? You have accomplished so very much. I'm sure Clara would be ever so proud of your achievements."

"Thank you, Cindy," Chris said equally soft. In light of their first conversation this was terrific even though it sounded over rehearsed.

Holly added, "And with all your other obligations, including caring for a sweet young daughter, you are still on the dean's top academic list. You have been inspiring."

Carter was smiling, but his head was shaking because he was still thinking about their previous conversation. He said in a worried voice, "I know you told me it was an investment, but did you really buy a house and a twenty seven acre commercial property? It takes me weeks to buy a new car and I need financing to do it. You spent four hours and paid cash for your purchases. It's none of my business but where does an enlisted man come up with all that money?"

As though he was asking a general question to those seated at the table, Cindy replied, "Well, they have all of Clara's insurance money. I'll bet that was burning a hole in their pockets."

Randall leaned toward Cindy, about to answer her ignorance when Chris beat him to it. "You are absolutely correct, Carter," she said sweetly. Randall looked at her face and noticed that there was not even a little hint of anger. "It is none of your business. Randall came into a very generous inheritance recently. In the spirit of romance and bridge building, he is taking better care of me and my projects than even you can imagine." Then looking at Cindy she said lightly, "As for Clara's insurance, it is in a trust fund in Julie's name, guaranteeing her education. You probably wouldn't understand that either."

Standing, Chris told Julie to give Grampa Jeff and Gram Holly a big hug. "It's time for us to beat feet to Chico and Rans is going to be on a very long flight to D.C.," she said brightly. "We'll keep you all updated."

Randall thought to himself, "She's not always kind, but she is gentle and for sure she is no pansy."

It was difficult to say goodbye after such an exciting week together. Chris and Julie were going home on an Alaska airline and Rans was flying on an American Airline. They shuffled through the security line knowing that they were going to different concourses. Julie was the first to shed tears. She clung to Randall even after he had promised he would return before Christmas.

"Do you cross your heart?" she said with a sad voice.

Rans lifted her so he could kiss her cheek and whisper in her ear, "I cross my heart. We can count the days together and I will call so we can talk before your bedtime every night."

She sniffed and replied, "You know a cross your heart promise is the very truest kind. I'll draw a happy picture of us together."

Before he put her down he said, "Very soon we won't have to worry about being apart. We'll be together every day. I'm very eager for that."

Chris joined the hug since she was a bit teary too. "We are very eager for that just as much. I'm sure Kenny Fox will probably have questions for us. I'll make sure to get your approval before we proceed." She gave him a little kiss.

As he lowered Julie he said gently, "I already approve of every idea you have for our projects. I am thrilled with your decision-making." He wrapped his arms around her and drew her gently against his body. "I so support your dream." A delightful kiss expressed their affection for one another and neither of them wanted it to end.

"Oh my," she said breathlessly. "I think I have something to add to my Christmas list. I hope Santa is listening." With another kiss, now the tears were happy ones as they went their separate ways.

"Oh, Rans, I'm so glad to hear your voice." She fairly sang and said "I know it has only been one day. But I have so much to tell you. But first Julie wants to tell you about her day at Kindergarten."

"Hi Daddy. Today in Miss Evans' class we made Reindeer posters with our feet." "Uh huh, she told us to step in the brown watercolor paint, and then step on a piece of art paper." "Yes, it was cold and I was careful not to smear." "Yup, some kids had to do it over." "It was really fun. She put two dots of tape on our paper before we stepped on it. When my paper was dry she helped me remove the little pieces of tape and put eyes where the dots were and then antlers. Did you know that they are not called horns? Yup, and both momma and daddy reindeer have them. We learned a lot about them." Several minutes of kindergarten facts were shared before she said, "Momma is telling me it's bedtime. May I talk to you some more tomorrow?" "I love you too."

When Chris finally reclaimed the phone she was grateful that Julie had felt the closeness of Rans and his availability. Now it was her turn. After just a bit of warm exchange she said, "Kenny has given a lot of attention to cleaning up the shambles at the house. He said that they have removed four truckloads of debris so far. There are some nice things, however, that didn't get messed up by the kids. There is a desk, leather furniture from the media room, There is a nice boat and motor in the garage. He said there was a lot that he didn't think should be thrown away so he is filling the garage. We can look at it the next time we are there. But he says it already looks tons better."

She listened as he reaffirmed his trust in both her and Kenny to make decisions about that sort of stuff. "Well I told him that I thought you would prefer hard wood floors," she said, "instead of carpeting. He said that was good because there was little carpeting left undamaged."

Her voice softened and she asked, "Do you have any hunch when your Christmas holiday is going to begin? How much longer must I go without seeing your face?"

He answered with a renewed voice, "That is the news I want to share with you. Colonel Sherman has his hair on fire to get a strike team reengaged ASAP. He also wants to spend the Christmas holiday in Bermuda. So as soon as I can get the guys organized, there is nothing keeping me here. He told me I'm free until the New Year. How about that?"

"That's way better news!" she answered. "When will you know so I can make some plans for us? She was trembling with excitement.

His voice got sort of quiet, like he was sharing a secret. "I have two committed; I just need a third. My best chance is your brother. If I can get a green light from him I can be there by Wednesday evening. Is the garage still available?"

"Oh yes," she breathed happily. "I've got a class until 2 tomorrow afternoon. You can call me from 1700." She nearly giggled, "Let's make plans!"

Not many folks had Michael's cell phone number, so when Randall dialed it he knew he was taking advantage of a privilege. It rang four times before he heard that familiar voice. "Hey Chief," he tried to sound casual. "It's Howe." He wanted to make it sound routine. "Are you busy for a couple days?"

"Randall, it's good to hear your voice, you old dog. I thought your hide would be tacked up on a barn somewhere by now. Are you still milkin' that nick on your leg?" They both chuckled.

"I miss you too, Mike. I want to thank you for the impromptu side track to St. Thomas. The doctor told me repeatedly that your quick decision saved my life. But this is not a social call. Colonel Paris Sherman has moved over into Homeland Security Special Ops and is trying to regroup part of the old strike team. That's a frustrating job because half of them are reassigned all over the world. He is in charge of information extrication. When folks take our secrets, he gets them back. Denny and Glen are the only available team members I can find. They need your help, Bro. They are all that are left of our team. Their hearts are as good as ever, but they need leadership, which you have in double portion. Have you got a couple days to go to Dubai?"

"You say Sherman is a full Colonel?" Michael asked trying to give himself a few moments of consideration.

"Yeah, we all get next grade; even though I have not been cleared for combat I get to sew Master stripes on my sleeve. If you will join them you'll get back pay to your separation date as a WO4. The target is a woman who was at the Patent Office. She copied a load of important innovations that could hurt us if it goes public, from military weapons, to pharmaceuticals, to new technology. The Chinese would love to get their hands on it."

There was a long pause before Michael asked, "Wouldn't it be SOP (standard operating procedure) to send in a team of Feds to bring her home?"

"Right." Randall agreed, "But we don't have a treaty with the Emirates, so we need to improvise." He could tell that Michael wanted to turn down the operation. "You don't have to kill her, just make her inoperable before she sells the stuff. Our intel is that she is squirreled up in a luxury hotel with some bodyguards and has invited a lot of bidders into her yard sale. It should be an easy in, easy out. Three days max." Before Michael could reply, Randall added, "There is an F-18 waiting for you at the 23rd Air Base at Portland International."

Michael smiled at his confidence. It wasn't the advancement of rank that had his attention, nor even the plea for assistance. If he could be honest with himself, there was a bit of the thrill of a challenge. He would be on a mission once more.

The operation began by turning off the power to the eleventh floor of the hotel, which opened all the solenoid locked doors. The first guard that tried to prevent them from entering was hit with a dart; the other two fell to Denny's .22. The screaming woman was quieted by another dart. Six hours later that naked woman, who had been heavily sedated, was trying to explain why she had no memory of the deaths of those three men, even though the pistol that took their lives was in her hand. Her chemically induced amnesia did not appear to be temporary. Without luggage, money, I.D, or most importantly, computer related items, she could not give them her name, nationality or her purpose for being in Dubai. Her room, including the safe, had been stripped of all contents. The

Bombardier Learjet from Dubai had Michael back in Portland in only eleven hours.

The base chapel was adorned for the season. Chaplain White had even placed a Christmas tree with white lights and ornaments. A purple wall banner had four candle shapes and the word Rejoice. It gave the room a happy atmosphere.

"Friends," the Chaplain began, "we have known Chris Meyers as a dedicated and courageous young woman who has committed herself to the Meyers family in a heroic manner. For the past seven years you have watched Jewel Meyers grow from a delightful child to become a lovely young lady. Some of you have had the privilege to meet Master Sergeant Randall Howe when he served the NSA and now is stationed with Homeland Security. It is our distinct honor this afternoon to join these three into a holy family guided and blessed by a loving God who calls us here and now joins with us in Jesus' name."

From the back of the room Perry Wilson and an obviously pregnant Sue Wilson walked slowly as best man and maid of honor witnesses. Julie entered right behind them carrying a satin pillow with three rings tied with a bow. The chaplain invited the seated group to rise and greet the bride and groom.

There was a brisk applause as Randall in his dress blues with new stripes and a chest full of service awards held his arm for Chris, who was dressed in a stylish blue two piece suit. In her hand were three red roses. Their wide smiles were a testament of joy in this precious moment.

The Chaplain spoke about the beauty and strength of a Christian home; then he read from Romans 12 the characteristics of building a holy marriage. When he asked Randall if he would take Chris as his bride, the groom answered, "Yes, forever." When Chris was asked if she would have Randall as her husband she answered, "Oh, yes I do." When Julie was asked if she would help make a happy home by honoring her mother and father, she answered, "Yes, I cross my heart I will."

The wedding couple had agreed to write their own vows and to keep them brief. Chris had said, "You don't need to promise me the moon, just mean every word you say and I'll do the same." Their vows were heartfelt and caused several tears to give evidence that the listeners were moved by them too.

Chaplain White removed the rings from the small cushion and after speaking about the beautiful symbols they represented he gave one to Randall. The groom placed the ring on Chris's finger saying, "Like God's love, this ring has no beginning or end. May you wear this for all to see the abiding love we have together. I pledge you my love as long as I live."

When Chris received the next one she said, "In receiving this ring I receive you as my husband." Then she slipped a ring on his finger saying, "I give you this wedding ring as another seal of our marriage. May it be a witness for the entire world to see our love! I pledge you my love as long as I live."

Randall replied, "In receiving this ring I do receive you as my bride." He then accepted the small third ring and he said as he placed it on the third finger of Julie's right hand, "Julie, this ring represents God's love for you as well as a father's and mother's abiding affection. As you grow you may wear it on a chain as a necklace. Wherever you go, however, know that our family's love is always with you." He bent and gave her a hug as Chris joined in the embrace.

When they finally stood, the chaplain removed the stole from around his neck and wrapped it around the hands of the bride and groom. "When the priest did this," he said happily, "the folks said that he was tying the knot. May you three go in wonder and joy, may you know the tender love of God who this day has made you a holy family, in Jesus name. Amen Now a kiss is the seal to it all." The folks stood and clapped their enthusiastic support.

The following hour was adorned with wedding traditions.

Perry took a lot of photos; there was cake of course; a table full of light snacks and either punch or champagne. Not many chose the punch. But everyone was eager to meet the groom and compliment them both for the tender service.

As the crowd was thinning, Chris informed Sue that Rans wanted to have supper at Ernie's Steak House again. "We need a moment to catch our breath and share one of their Imperial Chocolate Sundaes. We'll see you back at the house."

The table conversation began with a happy review of the brief wedding and its highpoints. Julie said she knew that the bride and groom were the main parts, but she felt very important too. She admired her ring again and again.

Chris admitted that she had few weddings to compare to theirs. "I was nervous at first, but quickly changed to just plain thrilled." She reached for his hand and added, "You are so handsome in your dress blues! Wow! Everyone there knows you are an outstanding Marine. Semper fi!" Then with a bit of a giggle she said, "And I get to take you home tonight."

For Julie there was little significance to that statement. After all, Rans had been a guest several times before. But for the married couple there was profound significance. "I've been thinking," Chris continued. "Your stuff is already in a travel bag. Wouldn't it be more practical to move that into my master bedroom? That is unless you have a lot of hair products and skin lotions that I don't know about." They both enjoyed her humor, grateful that a delicate decision was made that easily.

Sue's only advise to the bride-to-be had been, "On your wedding night you will feel shy of course. If you can be a little enthused and eager, it will encourage him and be a welcomed ice-breaker." It was advice that Chris tried to remember and apply. Do you know the old adage: "Act enthusiastic and you will be enthusiastic"? It really is true. Oh boy, is it ever!

Chris had prepared an apple casserole for Sunday morning. When the smiling newlyweds entered the kitchen there was the aroma from the oven and Perry and Sue were preparing bacon and scrambled eggs to go along with it. Sue asked, "So newlyweds, what are your plans for the week?" Obviously she expected a celebration honeymoon event.

Chris sighed and said, "Both Julie and I have school this week. I'm hoping I can get the golfers situated by Thursday so we can get back down to Orchards. Both projects are being blessed by dry weather." As an after-thought she asked, "Do your folks have Christmas plans? There is plenty of room for visitors."

Monday morning at 9:00 o'clock the phone rang. Randall was tempted to answer it since he was closest, but Chris picked it up with a smile. It was Ruth Justin from Washington's DSHS. "Good morning Mrs. Meyers, Mrs. Marshall informed me that you are buying a home in Orchards, Washington. If that is true I am delighted for several reasons. The main one is that I have a vacancy in my supervision staff that you could easily fill. There are six women's shelters in Cowlitz County that require oversight with a weekly visit and short report. The salary is sixty two thousand and car expenses." She paused waiting for a reply. When there was none she asked, "Does that sound interesting to you?"

"To tell you the truth, Mrs. Justin," Chris quietly answered, "that's about what I received as a nanny. I would hate to think that an MBA is worth so little."

The tactful lady laughed softly and said, "I totally agree. There was not much advancement possibilities as a nanny, however. With this starting point at DSHS there are unlimited opportunities. You are far too talented to remain there long. I can envision a bright future here. Will you at least think about it? I would love to have you on my team."

"I will think about it, Mrs. Justin. But I am also currently restoring a property in Vancouver to be a test model for my thesis. If I can get it going, I may be a contractor for you." Chris just liked the way that sounded.

Mrs. Justin knew when to push no further so she said, "If you can send me a copy of that thesis I would be happy to understand what has your interest."

Chris said warmly, "It's on the way. Thank you for this call this morning. I will consider your offer."

The Christmas Eve news had a heartwarming personal interest moment. The announcer's voice said happily, "Here's one that will warm you heart. Several shoppers at the Chico East Hills Shopping Center report receiving a greeting card from a total stranger. When they opened the card they were surprised to find a one hundred dollar bill and a card that said, 'Merry Christmas' with a scene of a baby in a manger. Inside it had a picture of a church and the words, 'And a Holy New Year.' Now that is the spirit of the season."

Julie had a big grin as she said, "I never knew that giving people a gift could be so fun." Looking at her daddy she finished the thought. "And doing it as a surprise made it twice as fun." Her mom and dad exchanged a happy smile and agreed whole heartedly.

Randall's return to D.C. was increasingly difficult. In fact it was only possible by daily phone calls and the promise of a four day weekend soon. Kenny was making wonderful progress, Chris reported. The officer's quarters had the new roof finished as well as a very large parking area in the front black topped. The foundation would be completed in another week. And the Orchards house had new windows and sliding doors installed. Painters were lined up to apply white ceilings and two shades of Periwinkle walls.

It was just before Valentine's Day when Randall used Michael's phone number again. "Good morning, Boss, it's your favorite cheer leader."

"Good to hear your voice again Master Sergeant. What has your hair on fire today?"

"Oh, you know the same old drill. They're trying to decide whether I'm 50 or 80 percent disabled. At any rate I'm still not cleared for combat and we have a situation. A Major thought he could help himself to a cute Second Lieutenant and assaulted her. She filed charges against him and rather than face his court marshal the fool fled to Vietnam, where there is no extradition treaty. He's living there like a happy prince charming. Col. Sherman doesn't care how it happens but he wants justice, quick and hard. Denny and Glen will once again be your fellow travelers. Can we count on you again? There's another F 18 waiting to take you to Travis Air Base."

"I don't know, pal, I've got a pretty full plate. I think I'll pass on this one," Michael said after a moment's thought.

"We both know this will get screwed up without you. It is nine month's pay for a three day drill. We really need you, Mike." Randall's voice was soft and convincing.

The trio caught up with the Major at a seaside resort. The happy hour crowd was already blustery when an unexplained riot started near the pool tables. A rush of attention to that part of the room prevented anyone from witnessing the dart and ice pick that ended the fugitive Major's life. Once again Col. Sherman would give high marks for the plan and execution of it.

Let's see; the next emergency was in March, when there were four of them close together.

Mr. Lee called to tell Chris that Mr. Edward's daughter was coming to attend school at UCLA and would assume all responsibility for the golfers. He thanked them for their reliable service and promised that a lovely drawing of Mt.

Fujiyama was on its way to express the agent's gratitude. "From this date the daughter will manage the details," they were told bluntly.

When Sue heard that news she immediately began to weep, declaring it a terrible shock and a horrible loss.

Chris asked her to take a deep breath and reconsider. "This might be a perfect blessing in disguise." When Sue shook her head in confusion, Chris said, "Your due date is just a month away. This would be a perfect time to rest and not fret about anything, the golfers especially. You can just get ready to welcome that baby." Now Sue nodded in agreement, but a tear still made its way down her cheek.

Finally Chris asked, "How much have you banked in nearly two years? I know how much I have put in the bank and it would easily be enough to purchase this place. You can comfortably live on what Perry earns at ATF." When Sue tried a weak smile, Chris continued, "I've been wondering about contacting some travel agents in Tokyo and Osaka. I'll bet they would love to get into the same deal we've been enjoying." Now there was an understanding nod from Sue. Seen in this new light the future didn't look so dim after all.

The second emergency was due to a message on her answering machine from Mrs. Justin. "Chris," she began, "I have just passed your thesis along to Craig Clark, a man Governor Gregoire has appointed as Secretary of Corrections. He is extremely interested in your model. If you are living in the Vancouver area, you could be a supervisor for us and a contractor for him. I don't want this to sound too urgent, but I really need to fill my vacancy. The women's shelters need guidance and support. This seems like an optimal opportunity for you. May we schedule a meeting in Orchards, to view the project there and give me a final answer?"

Chris answered her immediately because it fit so well in her plans. "I can meet with you next Friday at noon. My husband is arriving at Sea-Tac at 9 o'clock. We can meet you at the Salmon Creek Shari's there at the junction of I-5 and I-205. The project is framed out but still unfinished. At least you can see the scope of it and get an idea of its function. I'll pray about the supervisory position."

The third emergency was triggered by yet another phone call to Michael's personal number. "Sorry to rain on your parade, Bro, but we've got a real problem."

Michael could tell this was serious for there was none of the usual bantering before getting to the main course. "Don't we usually have a kiss and some sweet talk before you put the heavy stuff on me?"

Randall's voice was strained as he said, "Yeah I wish there was time for that. A Corporal at Fort Leavenworth hit the arsenal this morning, with an accomplice. They killed three guards and loaded a dozen rocket launchers and two dozen crates of rockets on a box truck. The accomplice was hit with a couple rounds during the scuffle. He lived long enough to tell us that the blue moving truck is headed for Canada. The plan is to load it on a Vancouver freighter bound for the Persian Gulf. Here's the rub. He's already got a twelve to fourteen hour jump on us. We're in Virginia and even with a jet, we couldn't catch up. He could be in your neck of the woods as we speak. We have alerted the Highway Patrol. But this isn't a sure thing or high on their priorities. Sherman wants this guy stopped cold. He doesn't want this to be a plea bargain or lengthy trial deal. If you can catch up with him it should go down without prejudice or consideration. He killed three of ours."

Michael finally had time to ask, "How will I identify the truck?"

"It's a blue International Box Truck with a Nebraska license and 'Mountain Movers' on the side doors. At night he could pretty easily slip across the border with a phony bill of lading. I hope you can prevent that from happening."

Michael drove north on I-5, going faster than trucks but aware that a weary driver might need a rest area. To make sure he didn't pass the blue truck Michael took a quick sweep through every rest area he came to, the one north of Vancouver, the one just past Kelso, the one near Olympia, the one south of Seattle. He wondered if this could possibly work. He drove slowly through the rest area north of Smokey Point and the one south of Bellingham. He was running out of opportunity and time. It was about midnight; that's when he saw it, parked over to the side with its lights off. He called Randall to report that he had the target in his sight.

"Take him down, man. Do not let that truck make it to Canada!" Randall's voice was strong and convincing. "Those rockets could deliver a lot of grief on our guys."

Michael made sure there was no one around to witness, then he knocked softly on the truck door. Speaking in a slurred voice like one who had too much to drink he ask, "Hey man, can you give me a ride home?" He knocked a little louder and heard a sleepy voice "Beat it, bum. I got nothing for you."

Michael knocked again, a bit louder. He was pretty sure that would do it. The driver side window slid down a bit, but it was enough for Michael to have a clear shot. A growling voice said. "Get the hell off my truck. The only thing you're going to get here is hurt!" He probably didn't hear the .22 round that hit him in the throat that also took out his spinal cord and certainly not the one an instant later when he was hit in the temple by a kill-shot. Wearing latex gloves, Michael reached in to unlock the door so he could roll up the window and relock the door. It would be a puzzle for whoever discovered him.

Back in his car, Michael called Randall to report a successful intervention and where authorities could catch up with the truck. Before he finished the call he said, "Tell Sherman I am no longer accepting another assignment. This one was too far over the line. I'm not his personal assassin regardless of the urgency or money. I've never felt as dirty as I do right now.

Cross my name off the list." He ended the call without saying farewell and Randall knew he was speaking the truth.

Randall also knew that it was way past time to find a righteous use of his time and he knew precisely where that could occur and with whom. He filled out his request for separation from the Corps on grounds of medical disability.

The fourth emergency was Monday morning March 20th. Perry had left for work early and suddenly Sue felt sharp pains. She told Chris that she thought the baby might be a bit early. Chris called Perry to meet them at the hospital because they were leaving immediately. Between groans of discomfort, Sue expressed her gratitude that Chris was such a gracious friend. It was good that Perry hurried because Clara Anne was born with just a couple hours of labor. Mom and baby did just fine on the first day of spring.

In Shari's Restaurant, Chris was making the introductions. "This is Randall Howe, my husband as of last Christmas. He was a Master Sergeant in the Marine Corps until just last week. A battle injury was severe enough to end his military career. Now he is all mine."

Mr. Clark, the Secretary of Corrections responded with a cheery voice, "No wonder you are so perky this morning. New bride, MBA graduate with honors and wrapping up a significant construction project. You are a shining star. I can see why Mrs. Justin is so eager to have you on her staff."

Mrs. Justin interjected, "Craig, you forgot to mention purchasing a new house here in Orchards. That in itself would be worthy of praise."

Rans and Chris exchanged a knowing smile because they had agreed on the drive down to be on guard for veiled probing questions. Chris said casually, "Well the praise may be a little slow in coming. The house was a bank repo that had major damage. We haven't seen the progress of repairs. We'll do that after we see the big project."

Mr. Clark asked after a long pause in the conversation, "Chris, tell me about your security plan for the project. That seemed unexamined in your thesis."

"That is one of the stark differences in this concept. There are no locked cells or armed guards so the residents of this facility would be low risk to start with." She glanced at Randall for encouragement. "Instead of a lock-up, my plan uses peer pressure. Each inmate will have a big sister sharing her room; perhaps someone who has been incarcerated long enough to have work release status. The big sister's purpose is to act as a monitor and share in the Second Chance opportunities of development. The heart of this effort is the reduction of the recidivism rate. If the inmate leaves the program prematurely and her big sister does not immediately report it, when she is apprehended both she and the big sister will be returned to general population with new charges and no opportunity for early parole. Someone from the waiting list will come to Second Chance and take her place. My bet is that it will only happen once or twice before folks understand the importance of their cooperation."

She thought for a moment then added, "Chapter eight of my thesis suggests more fully the concept of a philosophy of enhancement rather than enforcement as a security plan. There will be an attendant at a lobby desk of course; but her job is to report unauthorized absence and prevent unwelcomed guests from entering the house. With a houseful of young women, I can imagine that keeping sneaks out might be a more pressing challenge than keeping the inmates in."

Before Mr. Clark could ask another question, Mrs. Justin suggested that it would be more helpful to see the project than talk about it. Since there was nothing on the table but empty plates, her suggestion was eagerly accepted.

"It is only about ten minutes from here," Chris said happily. "Will you follow us?"

They found four large trucks in front of the building. An electrician was installing can lights, lots of them. A plumbing company was installing sinks and toilets in each room and four hot water heaters in the basement. The showers had already gone in. It was an invigorating sight to see all this action. Kenny Fox came out to greet them and when he was introduced to the two distinguished guests he offered a quick tour. He said he only had a few minutes because there was an old house that needed his attention too.

"I am impressed," Mr. Clark expressed again. "This seems more like a resort than a detention facility. I can see the effort to make this a bell-ringer as a model. You are preparing for a colossal success." Then he explained that Washington State currently has twelve prisons, ten for males and two for females. There are sixteen thousand inmates and another eleven hundred being housed in Michigan. There are sixteen work release facilities, to which this gem might be added. Fourteen of those are being operated by contractors, so there is already a precedent established. "Oh my, this is so impressive. None of our other facilities have this sort of charm!" he said again. "This easily will draw national attention, the sort of thing that makes a career." His intent was unspoken and his smile was genuine.

Thirty minutes later they were gathered in the parking area when Mr. Clark asked, "I didn't see much of a kitchen. Are you planning to use cooks?"

Chris smiled and replied "I think that was mentioned in chapter four. You must know that most state facilities now use Food Service of America to deliver meals and Liberty Distribution will supply as many vending machines as needed. We'll just use folks for dish washing and cleanup. I know that is mentioned in chapter three."

"Mrs. Howe, I am definitely impressed with your thoroughness," he said as they approached their car. "Tell me, have you had this work published or is it copyrighted?"

Chris thought that was a very strange question to ask, but she shrugged as she said, "No, this is my master's thesis. I was just fortunate to have an insightful mentor and a couple patient professors." Turning toward Mrs. Justin she added, "I am very interested in the supervisory position here. I'll know my availability as soon as I get back to Chico. May I call you?"

She told Kenny that she would follow him up to Aviary Avenue East.

On the way up the hill, Randall said, "You know, I don't trust that Clark guy. He seems like a shifty little weasel to me."

Chris nodded her agreement. "I couldn't understand why he asked about the copyright," she said thoughtfully.

"Is there some way he could leverage that away from you?" Rans joined in her questioning.

"Well I suppose he could block me from getting inmates to conduct the concept," she finally said. "But I can't imagine that would be beneficial to him. I feel like he wants to get some credit for the new direction of it." They were lost in thought until the pleasant new neighborhood changed their attention.

It was a completely different house that he showed them. All the damages were replaced or repaired, the exterior had been painted a formal gray with white trim and the lights were on. The twin oak doors looked both elegant and inviting. When Chris was shown the master bedroom with a huge window that overlooked the river and framed Mt. Hood, she wept. The house seemed to both Chris and Randall like some extravagant movie set.

Kenny guided them to the end of the east hall, which opened to the garage. "In the clean up," he said, as he pointed to a large collection of recovered items, "there was all this. You probably don't want all of it, but I'll wager there are a few treasures that you will choose to keep." They didn't spend much time examining the pile, but Rans saw enough to bring him back.

In the living room he pointed to the large fireplace. "Both up here and in the activity room there are wood burners. I wonder if you would prefer gas operated ones instead. This would be an easy time to install them."

Rans looked at Chris and when she nodded, he answered, "I'd love to flip a switch and not worry about smoking up the place."

"Come down to the basement," the contractor invited. "There are a couple questions I have there. I think you will be impressed again now that all the trash and trespassers are gone." They appreciated his humor with a bit of laughter.

He led them to the double sliding doors that looked out at the deck, or what was left of it. Someone had set fire to the open end of it. "I can replace the deck if you like. This is such a terrific view point. But for a bit more, we could pour a concrete wall and back-fill it so we can make a paver patio. With those doors open, it will really make a dramatic addition to the activity room."

"I really like the sound of that," Chris said. "How do you feel about that, Rans?" She was darling when she was enthused about something.

"Yeah," the big guy said. "I like that a lot more than a railing sort of thing that blocks this terrific view. Go for it."

"O.K. I've just got to ask you two something," Kenny said cautiously. "I'm pretty sure you are related to one of my other dear friends. Miss Chambers felt the same way. But you have never mentioned Michael Winter. He has a home just west of Portland. Is there some reason I should avoid the subject too?"

"That's a complicated question, Kenny," Chris said softly. "He is my brother but it has been over twenty years since we have seen one another. I was just five or six years old. Randall served with him for four years in the Marine Corps. I very much want to see him and build some wholesome family ties. I just want it to be the right time and way. I'd appreciate it very much if you just keep our secret. I think by the time our house is ready to let us move in we'll plan a big get together. Will you do that for us?"

"Yeah, I'll help in a surprise," the contractor grinned. "And I'll ask Miss Chambers to be in on it too because she sees him more often than I do, which is a lot. Now let me show you the last surprise I have about this house." He led them back into the activity room to the wall with a built in bookcase about five feet wide.

Chris looked at Rans to see if he understood something that she was missing and he just shrugged back.

Kenny said, "I spent several days in this place before I realized that this is about the end of the hallway upstairs and the wall into the garage. Does it seem to you that this bookshelf is unusual? I didn't think anything about it until I noticed this lever. I think this is a surprise under the shop area of the garage" His hand moved a section of what looked like trim, until he pulled it. The trim was a solenoid lever switch, which allowed the bookcase to swing back into a very large dark room.

Kenny reached in and flipped the switch that lighted a room lined with empty wine racks and three dusty card tables. Its size was at least twenty by thirty feet. "I'll bet the young couple who let this place go had no idea this was even here. It looks like it has been closed for a very long time. I wish it still held some of those bottles that were in here originally. I'll bet there were a lot of card games down here and a lot of cigars smoked that the ladies forbade in any other part of the house." He laughed, "Here is a man-cave for sure. Randall, do you like wine?"

"I've never developed an appreciation for it," the big guy said. "Now with this place, however, and a twenty seven acre hillside to grow grapes, I just may learn to like it," a grin punctuated his feelings.

They spent nearly an hour becoming familiar with the wonders of the house and making plans. Before they headed back to Seattle, Chris told Kenny that she thought a little girl would appreciate a white and pink bedroom.

Randall was nodding his approval too. He quietly said, "I appreciate everything I've seen today. You've done an outstanding job Kenny." He handed the contractor a travel kit saying, "I paid the bank, but you have been carrying this project from the get-go. I'm pretty sure there is a hundred thousand in here. Whenever you need the rest just give me a shout. My new address is Chico." There was a sense of satisfaction shared by them all.

There were no emergencies in April but quite a bit of accomplishment:

The Chico house was appraised and Perry said it was not enough. They would pay an additional five thousand for the furnishings.

Two Japanese travel agents responded immediately to Chris's plan for golfers. She set them up for alternating weeks and knew the opportunity would grow as large as Sue wanted. Chris made it clear that she would be too busy to be involved in this one.

Kenny was finished with the Second Chance and Chris requested approval from the Secretary of Corrections to begin screening for program inmates. After two weeks she was denied on the basis that the sprinkler system lacked current inspection tags.

Kenny finished the short punch list for the house and gave Chris a referral access to the wholesale furnishing company his company used. "I can give you three good reasons to use them," he said. "They are high quality wholesale, they deliver within twenty miles and in Oregon you pay no sales tax." Rans and Chris made several trips with enough cash to finish the redemption of a magnificent home.

Chris requested approval from the Secretary of Corrections

and after three weeks was denied again. This time due to inadequate fire extinguishers.

Chris closed her bank accounts at Sierra National and Cornerstone Federal and removed an awesome bundle of Treasuries.

Finally they moved from Chico with some sadness and much more joy. With three weeks left in the school year, Julie was allowed to attend the kindergarten class at Endeavor Elementary so she would get to know at least some of the boys and girls who would be with her in the first grade. They traded the Taurus in for a Chrysler 300 and Rans was convinced he was healed enough to drive a new Chrysler Pacifica.

Chris applied again for approval and after three weeks a third rejection letter explained that the doors were too narrow for fire safety.

Yes there were no emergencies but wasn't it a month full of important stuff?

Chris answered her cell phone. The personal assistant told her that the Secretary of Correction wished a phone conference. After a brief pause, Chris heard Mr. Clark's voice. "Good morning, Mrs. Howe. I haven't received another request from you and am curious about the status of Second Chance."

"Hello Mr. Secretary. I have not submitted a request because I have better things to do than play hide and go seek with a bureaucrat." There was no anger in the words but they stung the listener none the less.

"Oh my. That sounds serious. Have I given you cause to rethink your project?" His voice had an oily calm that caused her to intentionally take a calming breath.

"Oh no, sir," she said softly. "After three rejections over fictitious reasons I opened the possibility for other uses of the project. The director of procurement of the Economy Lodge has given me an initial offer to purchase the project for eight hundred fifty thousand dollars," she lied. "I think they will go higher. That was just their first offer. They will complete the kitchen and have a small restaurant to serve their guests as well as the local folks. It is such a great opportunity for us."

There was only silence until Mr. Clark said quietly, "I'm stunned. I thought we had an agreement. Those were only small items of requirement. I can't believe you would turn such an altruistic effort into a commercial one."

"Yup," Chris said a bit more final. "And when word gets around that the Secretary of Corrections fumbled a great opportunity again, because he had personal plans to take credit for the model, there might be even more shock in Olympia."

"Wait," he said. "That's pretty harsh. I didn't..." he stammered. "I wasn't..." There was a long pause before he quietly said, "What can I do to get our plan back on track." He was trying tactfully to regain control of a matter that he really wanted.

Chris said softly, "It is very evident that you do not want me to be a contractor in this effort. That's fine by me because I have already received my accomplishment of the thesis and I already have a full plate, as they say. If you want Second Chance and will use it for its planned intent, you may offer me a million one for it and be advised that the twenty four acre parcel behind it has been removed from the title."

"That is preposterous" he growled. "There is no way that it will appraise for that." Now his voice was becoming desperate.

Chris said, "Have a good day, Mr. Clark. Remember, you called me." And she hung up on him.

Two hours later Mr. Clark called back to say that he had found support for the purchase. "May we spread the payments over a three year period?" he was still trying to soften the loss of face.

"Of course you can, sir. There will be a ten percent interest rate on the unpaid balance however. Do I look like a mortgage lender?" Her nature would have been more agreeable had it not been for his shifty initial approach.

"Northwest Title Company," he said curtly, "will contact you when documents are ready to be signed and you can receive the total amount. It will take a couple weeks to make arrangements." Now his voice was resigned to defeat.

In the dark of their room, she spooned against Rans. In a raspy voice that surprised herself she said, "I did today the very thing that upset me when you made a decision without me. I didn't plan on selling the Second Chance without you. His greasy attitude caused me to express my disregard and suddenly he was in a corner. I'm so sorry for doing that."

Rans turned over so he could stroke her cheek. "I'm not saying that it was unimportant, but I do feel it demonstrates that we are a team. I don't want you to feel a need for my support unless the task is large enough for both of us. It sounds to me that you were quite efficient. I'm happy with the outcome. I just wish I could have seen his face." There was a bit of silence as she stroked his chest. "Does he understand that the property has been separated?" Rans asked .

Softly she replied, "I think that's what triggered his desperation. He said it was preposterous. My hunch is that he had personal plans that got way-laid. It felt good" She moved in a way that ended their conversation. Yeah, it felt real good.

As soon as school was out for the summer they took a three day excursion along the Oregon beaches. All three agreed it was beautiful but the water was way too cold to play in. When they were home Chris invited six of the girls from Julie's class to a peanut butter sandwiches and ice cream lunch. They watched a Marmaduke video while the moms got to see the restored home and chatted. It was a great way to meet a few of their neighbors.

Just before supper, Ran's phone rang. When he looked at

caller ID, he whispered as though the caller could hear, "It's Mike, your brother!"

"Hey Boss, I'm surprised you still have my number," Rans said enthusiastically. "Are things so slow in Portland you need a little mission exercise or maybe some extra cash?"

"No pal," that familiar voice said, "I'm getting plenty of exercise, and I don't need a job on the side. It is really good to hear your voice though. Are you pretty much patched up?" They did the ice breaker two step until finally Michael asked, "Are you still able to access the Defense Department files?"

Randall was a bit slow to answer, but finally said, "Yeah, I can do that unless they changed my password recently. Who do you want me to look up for you? You must have some private action going on." He hoped his copied discs could still get him in the system.

"You're right about that, bro," Michael said. "There is an Aloha cop that has triggered my bomb dog on two separate occasions. On top of that there have been three or four arson fires in churches of the area. This cop rubs me wrong. I just wonder if we have any file for a D. J. Stanton from Hillsboro Oregon. I haven't been able to get any listing for him from the directory and I don't want to make him suspicious. You've got my number if you run onto any intel."

To keep the conversation friendly, Michael asked, "Hey bro, are you any closer to getting that dance studio you kept talking about? I'm telling you, we've got some space if you want to get it started. There is already a lady here who is teaching tap dance lessons."

Randall said more seriously, "You've got a bomb dog? Damn I wish I had one of those." He was still for a moment then admitted, "Having a girl close enough to smell is probably a thing of the past. As much as I hate to let that dream go, I still need to wear a leg brace. I think the samba is out of the question."

In a matching voice Michael said, "I'm sorry to hear that.

Seriously, I'd like to see your ugly mug. I miss you, brother."
Michael was sure that if Stanton was in the system, there
would be ample information.

Julie asked if they could drive to Grampa Jeff and Gram Holly's
for a short visit. It turned into a fun overnight. By the time
Rans could get to his computer it was late Sunday evening.
Finally, Monday morning Randall returned Michael's request
for information.

"Hey Mike, you called it on this character. The Army had
a Dennis Justin Stanton who was section 8 out of the service in
'94." He gave Michael a Hillsboro address. "He was involved
in two arson fire investigations that could never be proven.
A warehouse and an Elks Club burned under suspicious
circumstances. When he set fire to a Camp Pendleton hillside,
however, there were witnesses. The fire was contained before
it got out of control but it was enough for him to be sectioned
out. There seems to be a lengthy list of part time watchman,
security sort of jobs. I can't figure out how he got past a
background check from a reliable police hire, unless he buried
his Army records under a couple dozen rent-a-cops. There
is no record of arrests or warrants. He's just a very unstable
person. Be careful, man; you know the sections can go off for
the littlest reason.

"Now about catching up with one another; I'm going to
be in Seattle next month. Do you have a vacancy I can hang
with for a couple days? I want to see Noell again. Man, she
was some kind of cute. I'll give you a shout in a couple weeks
for the details."

Compared to the Chico Base chapel the Good Shepherd
Presbyterian Church was quite large. They had heard from
several that the pastor, Gail Wesley, was outstanding. As the
three new folks found their seats they were surprised to be
joined by two of the moms who had brought their daughters

to Julie's party. They all sat together until the pastor invited the children to come up for a story time. Julie looked at her mom for permission and was happy to go along with her new friends.

The pastor was glad to welcome them and began a story about a little boy who watched his mother pour the very last of the baking flour into a bowl. "He loved the smell of baking bread," she said happily, "and was eager to taste the warm fresh delight. Now the mother had learned that their neighbor had been very ill and could not work. There was no money for food and so their table would be empty. But the boy saw two big loaves come out of the oven. He could hardly wait. With butter and perhaps a bit of berry jam...mmm... It made his mouth water." The pastor was an excellent storyteller and all the children could practically smell the baking bread.

"When the two big loaves were cool he was ready for a slice when his mother asked him to take one of the golden brown delights next door to help their neighbor. He thought to himself, 'No! Now there won't be enough for a snack, for a buttery slice with supper. There won't be toast for breakfast or sandwiches for lunch.' He didn't want to do it, but he did as he had been told and he saw the light of gratitude on their faces. The mom wept she was so happy to have some food for her family. She thanked him again and again.

"To the boy's surprise," the pastor spoke confidentially, "he had a warm bread snack when he got home and a slice for supper. There was toast in the morning and sandwiches for lunch. Perhaps his mother had sliced it a bit thinner than usual but there was plenty to go around and soon his pantry flour jar was refilled. He learned an important lesson. When we share with those in need there is enough to go around and our heart and theirs are happy."

The rest of the worship service was also uplifting and the music was inspiring. To complete their pleasant introduction to the church one of the moms invited them to a backyard barbeque where they would meet more of Julie's classmates.

"This reminds me of our church back home," Randall said quietly as a large smile expressed his gratitude.

One of the other summertime opportunities was a ten week adult program at Portland Community College. The Oregon State Extension catalogue had several really interesting classes, which Randall was browsing at the breakfast table. "I don't know which one I would choose," he said. "I think I need a class in engine maintenance, but it would be more fun to get into boat building."

"Which reminds me," Chris said cheerfully. "Do you have any plans for the boat in the garage? I've wondered about that one."

"You know," Rans sounded like he was recalling something important. "Tom, our yard guy told me that his brother owns a nursery and would love to barter for it."

She was more interested in the idea. "What would he trade for it?"

Rans shrugged, "I don't know the names of landscape flowers. But he should be here tomorrow. I can ask him now that I know you like the idea." He paused before asking, "What classes have caught your interest?"

"There's a Mother Daughter Quilt Making class that would be fun, and so would the couples cooking class be entertaining."

He continued to leaf through the pages. "Hey, here's one on Oenology."

"What the heck is that?" she asked playfully. "Is it about owning stuff? We are already doing a lot of that."

Rans grinned as he answered, "It must be the formal name for winemaking. It says, 'hobby to career' information. I think it would be fun to make something I could put in our secret room downstairs. Let's do it!"

She got a shy smile before she asked, "Could I ask you to do something sort of sneaky today?"

Rans was pretty sure she wasn't thinking about that, but she sure had his interest. "What would you like me to do?" he asked in a soft voice.

Chris said, "I would like you to contact Michael. He said he would like to see you. Will you call him. Tell him you are just passing through and would like to see him again." Her smile said she knew she had teased him and turned it into a mission.

"That's a whole bunch more scary than what I had in mind," Rans chuckled. "He is the most observant person I know. I'll need to take a taxi, wear my camos and no wedding ring, and pray to heaven that I have not gained weight in the last few months. He will probably want me to spend the night. Do you still want me to do it?"

Randall pressed the doorbell and heard Michael's happy voice say, "Welcome Bubba! Come on in and take the elevator up." There were only two floors so when the elevator doors opened Michael met him with a very large service dog.

As Michael embraced him he said, "Gabe was the service dog assigned to Noell's brother, a navy corpsman in Iraq. An IED ended their military service. Paul is an intern in a local hospital and Gabe is my shadow."

Randall asked as he noticed the absence of an ear and eye, "Is he the one who identified the problematic cop?"

"One and the same," Michael answered.

As they were walking toward double doors, Randall asked, "Did anything come of that guy? How did that work out?"

Michael shook his head. "You know he was a worse bomb maker than cop. An unexplained explosion took him and his house to another zip code." Randall nodded in understanding.

A smiling Noell joined them and Randall said politely, "We only met briefly in Coronado. It makes meeting you again and seeing this amazing home all the sweeter."

"These are our children," her voice was warm with pride, "Caleb loves the piano, Cam and Cele are the violinists. We've never had an opportunity to tell you, Randall, how blessed we have become because of your courage on that dark night. We couldn't be safer or happier. Thank you." She guided a tour of the home while Michael added information about their efforts here at Harmony House. All the while Gabe stayed right beside Randall. Perhaps it was the camos. But more likely it was the leg brace and limp that told him that here was another wounded comrade.

Before supper the kids gave a brief demonstration of their talent including a clever tuning run by the violins. Rans attributed the joyful feeling he experienced to his admiration of Michael and maybe a bit of envy of this amazing home. They even had a food center cook who had available Snicker Doodle cookies.

In the morning he didn't think about the pain in his leg. Only after he had shaved and showered did it occur to him that the pain was gone. He would still wear his brace, but honestly, he felt it was unnecessary.

The house was so quiet he was startled to find Noell in the kitchen. As she poured him a cup of coffee he learned that Michael and Gabe were out on a morning constitutional. Randall asked if the place was always this quiet.

After a brief listen, she answered, "During the school year they are up early. Since their rooms are interior ones they don't get a lot of street noise, although set back as we are, there isn't a whole bunch of that. It's nice and quiet wouldn't you agree?"

"Whatever it is," he replied, "I feel more rested than I have in months. Thank you for gracious hospitality."

Michael and Gabe returned and the sound volume increased. The kids were probably waiting for that signal because all three of them came out of their rooms still in pajamas.

"Oh, no you don't," Noell scolded. "You know the rule. Get dressed before you come to the table." Randall smiled because it was a typical wonderful family.

Michael asked about his plan for the day and Randall said, "I have an appointment with a Coronado realtor at 1600. He has found another place for me to consider." That was true. "I still have some incidentals to retrieve." That was not. "My flight out is at 1030." Neither was that. When Michael offered to drive him to the airport, Rans said that he had already called for a 0900 taxi. That was true. "But this has been such a wonderful time with you all, I wonder if I could stop by on my way to Vancouver in September? I've never been in Canada."

"You know," Michael said warmly, "you are always welcome here. If you want to leave from Seattle, there is a float plane service from Lake Union to Victoria or the clipper, which is a hydrofoil. It's pretty easy to fall in love with this part of the country." Randall nodded thinking of the two ladies in his life just across the river.

"Well, my Corps days are over for sure. I can't imagine another decade at a desk. Sherman is more and more involved with his political future and I darned sure want none of that. You all seem to have found a double portion of happy. It seems like a model I would be honored to follow." That was true too.

"No, Sweetheart," Rans shook his head, "he never mentioned his family at all. Noell has a younger brother that is living with them as he completes his medical school. I think she has another brother but he was never in a conversation. Her folks are in Minneapolis, and Michael never mentioned any relatives. Their house looks like a commercial building. It has an auditorium bigger than the church's that is used for the kid's music programs. It sounds like a lot of kids use it. The living area is the whole second floor and felt luxurious and friendly at the same time. I liked it a lot."

After a thoughtful moment he went on, "I'll tell you this. I can't remember him ever being happier than the Michael I saw, and softer than can be. He is one happy man."

It was a very busy summer. There were two trips to Seattle, one to see Gram Holly and one to introduce Rans to her brother Ward. They joined the church and invited the new member class to their home for a spaghetti dinner and Yahtzee tournament. Folks had such a good time they agreed to meet monthly for potluck supper and study. Three of the fellows invited Randall to join them for an Ilwaco salmon charter. He brought home two gorgeous salmon. He wrote to his dad saying the next time he feels like fishing, please come to the place where real fish are caught. All the while they were adjusting to a new life in Orchards.

Randall returned to Aloha in September saying that the life Michael had found was just what he had dreamed of. "I can't get this place out of my mind," Randall said respectfully. "I love listening to the kids make music. I think this is the sweetest town I can remember. I even drove over to the coast and fell in love with the beaches. Bro, I don't want to disrespect you so can you help me find a place somewhere nearby?"

"There is no disrespect," Michael said softly, "in a compliment, pal. Jump in the car with me and let me introduce you to Cherry Grove. It's about fifteen minutes from here and I think it will ring your bell."

As they were leaving church, Pastor Gail asked if she could come over some evening to talk about a special need the church had. Chris told her Friday evening was available. "We're taking extension classes right now," she explained.

"I'll try to use our time well," the pastor said with a big smile.

All week long they tried to guess what the need might be that would cause a busy woman to make a Friday evening appointment. Chris had a suspicious frown when she asked, "Do you have some dark secret that I don't know about?"

Her playfulness caused Rans to answer, "Well, I have been looking at another Coronado Island rental." That got him poked in the ribs, but only gently.

The pastor was surprised at the size and quality of this house for three people. She thought there had to be an interesting back-story, but was focused enough to stay on task. "One of our major outreach ministries is our commitment to Doctors Without Borders. Have you heard about them?"

Chris nodded and asked, "Isn't that a nondenominational mission?"

When the pastor assured her that she was correct, she continued, "Our church is not as restricted to where we make our priorities as some Presbyterian churches. We believe it is better to help what is already doing a wonderful ministry than reinventing something less." Both Chris and Randall nodded in agreement.

Looking at Randall she said, "Am I correct in believing that you were a Master Sergeant in the Marine Corps?" He nodded. "That is so much more impressive than a bunch of letters behind a name." Her words were pure respect. "Mr. Howe, you have already found several admirers in our church who think you are an effective leader. They have asked me to invite you to join the procurement committee for the Doctor's fund raiser in November. To tell you the truth they are the smallest and most efficient group I have in the church. Your task would be to find items or services that the dinner folks will bid on. It would also be to support the other six men who have already been working at generating an exciting catalog.

Realistically you would probably find your pace for next year. Does this sound like something that interests you?"

"Yes it does," he answered immediately. "I would be doing something that is crucially needed in oppressed areas or times of emergency. More than that, I would be meeting with men of achievement. It doesn't get much better than that." He thought for a moment then asked, "Where and when do they meet."

The smiling pastor answered, "They meet on the first Thursday morning of the month at 11:45 at the Charthouse. They have no program or other agenda so promptness is a priority with them."

"I like them more already," Randall said.

When it finally rolled around, Rans recognized one of two men standing in the restaurant lobby. After introductions, he was told that the other four were already seated. Randall smiled because they were not only prompt, they were early. Semper fi!

He took a few notes as each man shared their accomplishments. When it was his turn, Rans said, "I'm just honored to be included by you all. I've had a couple days to work on this so let me ask, would a whole bathroom remodel be an item of interest. The Multnomah Construction folks would offer that and set a value at $20k. Would four tickets to the Canadian Tenors row 3 center isle for the Saturday December 18th sold out concert, with a backstage after-party be a biddable item? I have no history on what you have done before so would a five course seafood dinner for four cooked by executive chef Len Harper from the Stafford Hotel at either the bidder's home or mine be interesting? He would bring two assistants for serving." Randall shrugged and said, "It was the best I could do in three days. We're new to the area." The other six broke into laughter. He had chatted with Kenny and they agreed on that price of a bathroom reno. Randall was paying for the donation. He would also be the high bidder on the tenors. That was a thank you he had planned to give Kenny for the splendid work on the house. He would still give it. The chef was to be a surprise for Chris. Depending on the bid, it still would be.

Randall looked at Michael impatiently saying, "No man, I'm not kidding. My vintner has said this is an ideal eco-zone to grow Viognier grapes. We planted the fifty original acres with Chardonnay next to the old Zinfandel, but this is more rocky. It's drier and they will make terrific wine. I'm serious. The house is not for a residence, but will be a terrific tasting room and wine store. I'll pay you for all the land you have up this hillside."

Michael had tried to explain that facing east it would get great morning sun but little in the afternoon and on the lee side of the hill there would be little rain. He wondered if Randall was getting rid of his confiscated cash too, so he finally said, "O.K. I look forward to some of this fractured wine."

The Youth Symphony Christmas sing-a-long was a huge success. They had requests for the free tickets that filled the auditorium on two nights. It was more delightful than anyone could imagine. Once again Mr. Klein distributed T-shirts. For the first night they were green with white letters and red with white letters for the second night. As the second night folks were cheerily exiting Michael and Noell were in the foyer chatting with folks. There were so many who wanted to thank them or compliment the youth program.

A patient lady with a daughter stood by the wall waiting for an opportunity to speak with them. Finally there was enough of a lull that she stepped up to Michael and offered her hand saying, "This was an amazing evening! I haven't had this much Christmas spirit since I was a little girl. I'm Crystal."

Michael smiled broadly and said, "This is our first attempt at a sing-along and it worked out much better than expected." Looking at the young girl he asked, "Who is this young lady?"

"This is Julie," Chris answered with pride. "She was blown away by how many talented kids were here. Are any of them yours?"

Noell answered, "The young man on the piano is Caleb, and the first and second violins are Cam and Cele. They are ours."

Michael asked Julie, "Do you play an instrument? Would you like to be a part of the orchestra?"

Crystal laughed softly, "She would love to be able to take lessons, but we don't have a piano."

She might have said more but Michael asked, "You look real familiar to me. This is my wife Noell. Have we met before?"

"I've heard I look a lot like my mom," Chris said brightly. "I think you knew her. But we were just kids." When he shook his head in confusion, she continued, "In the birth order I was in the middle. I was in trouble a lot with the creeps that mom brought home. There was a detention before the shelter home. Then I met the Meyers; Bruce was a helicopter pilot. When he was killed I used the insurance money to finish school. Now I'm the director of the Cowlitz Women's Shelters."

Michael was processing all this information more slowly than it was coming at him. He was wondering why this woman was trying so hard to get her daughter into the Aloha program.

Crystal shrugged in frustration. "I have an older brother who lives in the Portland area and a younger brother who lives in Seattle. Stars and little fishes, I don't know how to make it much clearer without spilling everything. Seven years ago you guys each put a snow job on the other. You accepted the notion that Ward was a custodian in an AIDs clinic, and he thought you were some hairy street bum trying to hustle some cash. There went more years of missed family. My birth name was Christina, which I changed when I married Bruce. For crying out loud", her voice carried a tinge of frustration, "I'm your sister."

While that was soaking in, Noell stepped over and hugged her sincerely. "Oh Sweetie, I've never had a sister!" she said with a sob. "Thank you for finding us."

Michael wrapped his arms around both of them and finally said, "Stars and little fishes, we have a lot of catching-up to do. I know a winemaker who would love to meet you."

Chris asked, now with a much softer voice, "Does he sort of look like that big guy standing near the door?" She pointed at a man who was immediately recognized.

"What the hell? That's Randall Howe," Michael murmured.

"Yup. We've got you surrounded. There is even more surprise in this evening," she said with a giggle. She was watching three other folks walk toward him.

"Michael, may I introduce your little brother Ward, his wife Becky and their daughter Sophie? They live in Seattle's Greenlake neighborhood. He's the Roosevelt High School Assistant Principal." Hugs and comprehension continued to grow.

From the exiting crowd Kenny and his wife Cheryl joined the circle and finally Lisle Chambers completed the happy crowd. It seemed that Michael was just beginning to understand what was happening. "Stars and little fishes," he growled, "who planned this ambush?" He didn't want to admit that he had been so completely surprised, and most certainly that he was enjoying it immensely.

Finally engaging as a hostess, Noell invited everyone upstairs where she had prepared a dessert for the children. Cheryl, dependable Cheryl, had also prepared an apple crisp for the rest of the crowd

For a while there was a lot of chatting and laughter. Finally Michael asked, "How the heck did this get put together?"

Randall raised his hand. "Denny and I were fishing for trouble when we went to the Chico house checking on a river of Japanese tourists. Chris said 'Stars and little fishes' and I was hooked. That was before the Puerto Rico raid. She was my angel of recovery."

Ward was seated next to him so he added, "I am host to some local GOP neighborhood meetings. Chris attended with Julie's grandmother and recognized me."

Kenny raised his hand and added, "They came to examine the old officer's quarters in Orchards. That's where we recognized the family resemblance."

Lisle added, "When I shook her hand it was unmistakably confirmed."

Chris said, "I asked Rans to fake a reunion with you and determine if we might be welcome. I didn't want a repeat of you guys conning each other.

"I feel like Christmas has come early this year," Michael said with obvious emotion. "We have a lot to talk about."

Noell invited folks to coffee, cake or a bit of wine if there were any takers. For several minutes there was the buzz of individual conversations. At the side of the room Sophie and Julie were meeting their big cousins, while Noell and Lisle spoke quietly. "Has everyone had a chance to refresh?" their hostess asked. "I'd like to do a test. I believe this time and place is uniquely filled with the presence and power of a Mighty God. Shall we see?" It was her house. Who was about to say "no"?

She brought out a box with a bunch of candles and holders. One by one she placed ten candles on the coffee table, two circles, one within the other. "Now Caleb, would you kneel down by that one," she pointed. He followed her instruction. The men were mystified, but wise enough to quietly watch. "Now Cam, kneel by the candle next to Caleb." "Now Julie, Honey, will you kneel down by Cam?" "Now Sophie," she didn't need to finish her instructions because the girls were going to the proper candles.

Noel got a lighter and carefully lit all ten candles then turned out the house lights. Softly she said, "This is an experiment in family solidarity and God's powerful hand at work within us." She paused before saying, "Now, Lisle, will you stand behind Cam?" The silent woman took her place. "Chris stand behind Julie; Becky stand behind Sophie and Cheryl stand behind Cele." She took her place behind Caleb and reached for the hands of the women on each side. The children were watching and followed her example. In a whisper Noell said "We are the circle and we are gathered in the presence of God's abiding love. In the mystery of the Holy Spirit we join our hearts as one."

Noell once again spoke softly, "Caleb repeat these words. 'I am courage'." The lad replied in an equally soft voice, "I am courage." The candle flame before him flickered and grew brighter. "Cam, say, 'I am Fidelity'." The words were repeated and again the candle brightened. "Julie, say 'I am Mercy'." The words were repeated and the light became brighter. "Sophie repeat, 'I am Wisdom'." The words were soft but repeated perfectly. "Cele, repeat, 'I am Compassion'." As she did, all the candles burned even brighter and Noell directed, "Hold on to each other's hands and bend way back. Look at the ceiling. There is a star within a star, five within five." As her directions were followed they all could clearly see it in the ceiling shadows, a star within a star.

Noell said, "Our circle has power of the Divine; power to bless, power to guide, power to heal, power to learn, and power to assist. We are five within five. God's Ageless Presence is a wonderful thing." After a moment's reflection, she said, "You may stand up and let go of the other hands, if you want to." She turned on the lights and the candles began to go out, one by one.

Noell said with a growing smile, "I have only one more bit of information tonight." Looking at Julie she announced "Honey, you are going to have a brother next summer." A startled Chris and Randall looked at each other. This is a wonderful thing indeed!

There is so much more story to tell; would that we had time to tell it!

Full Moon

The moon is full and dear to me,
        even in the shadow of a tree;
Its voice I've heard in the ethereal tune
        of the calling of a lonely loon;
I have often walked with him
        in the twilight warm and dim;
Tender Moon, you are there,
        patient in the rain-scented air.
I have looked for you at night,
        in the silent silver light;
I have seen your footsteps go
        softly over fallen snow;
Full Moon love is near for it is found
        as all precious things abound.
Hill or cloud, on leaf or star,
        Full Moon is never far. I adore you!

Printed in the United States
By Bookmasters